SMITTEN

WITH CAVIAR

SMITTEN

WITH CAVIAR

A SWEET ROMANTIC COMEDY

SET IN MONACO

ELLEN JACOBSON

Print ISBN: 978-1-951495-60-2
Digital ISBN: 978-1-951495-50-3
Large Print ISBN: 978-1-951495-59-6

Editor: Lisa Lee Editing
Cover Design: Melody Jeffries Design

First Printing: July 2024

Published by: Ellen Jacobson
www.ellenjacobsonauthor.com

For everyone who's geeked out over a
famous musician

CONTENTS

CHAPTER 1
CHAMPAGNE AND CAVIAR

"Be cool, Jasmine," I say to myself as the taxi pulls up in front of the Monte Carlo Casino. The palm trees lined in front of the casino sway in the light summer breeze, their movement mirroring the churning feeling in my stomach. Steeling my nerves, I tell myself, "Act like you belong."

After paying the fare, I adjust the straps of my cocktail dress. The silky material feels luxurious against my fingertips. I only hope it looks as high-end as it feels. Bargain basement steals are great when it comes to keeping your credit card debt at a reasonable level. Not so much when you're about to enter one of the most exclusive casinos in Europe.

One thing I do know about this dress is that the red color is striking against my dark hair and eyes. I'm so used to wearing only black when I perform with the Fjura Quartet that this dress feels bold in comparison. Like it wants me to be the center of attention for once, not my violin.

Actually, maybe that's what feels strange. Instead of carrying my violin case, I have an evening bag in my hands. Instead of trying to quiet my nerves before a performance, I'm trying to work up the courage to meet my blind date at a swanky bar. But if you're going to go on a blind date, this is the way to do it. A handsome rich guy and champagne and caviar await.

As I approach the entrance to the casino, three retirement-age women push past me. They're obviously American from their accents–one is from the Deep South, one from New York City, and the other one from somewhere in the Midwest.

A bouncer stops them. "I'm sorry, ladies, but tourists can only visit the casino between ten and one."

The woman from the Big Apple cocks her head to one side. "What makes you think we're tourists?" she asks, her voice thick with disdain.

I want to point out the obvious—one of them is snapping pictures with her camera, the other has a travel wallet hanging from her neck, and the third is wearing a t-shirt which says "Silver Fox on the Loose".

I stifle a laugh as I make eye contact with the bouncer. He gives me an appreciative look before turning back to the older ladies. "I'm sorry, but you'll have to come back tomorrow."

The southern lady tries to sweet talk him. "Now, hon, I don't mean to tell you how to do your job, but we've got money and we're here to gamble."

While the bouncer explains the dress code, I inch forward. Speaking in French, I tell the bouncer that I'm meeting my date at the Bar Salle Blanche. He nods, then holds open the door for me to enter.

I hear the women whispering to themselves about how snooty Parisian women are. If only they knew I was born and raised in a small American town. Sure, I had learned some French while studying at a conservatory in Strasbourg during a semester abroad in college, but I was far from fluent.

My jaw drops as I walk inside the atrium of the casino. Knowing the building had been designed in an opulent Belle Époque style is one thing. Seeing the marble columns, gilded stucco, colorful frescoes, and ornate sculptures in person is another. It's clear why this is one of the most luxurious destinations in Europe. The magnificence of the architecture is matched only by the glamorous dresses the ladies are wearing and the cool sophistication of the men accompanying them.

As I'm reminding myself yet again to play it cool, my phone buzzes. I frown as I read my blind date's text.

Business meeting running late. Be there soon. Meet you

at the bar.

I feel a wave of anxiety wash over me. Even though I'm outgoing and extroverted by nature, I hate going to places alone. Sitting at a bar by myself feels awkward, to say the least.

Steeling my nerves, I make my way to the bar. When I mention my date's name to the hostess, I'm immediately whisked to a table near the stunning hand-crafted mosaic bar. As I take my seat, my phone buzzes again.

Closed the deal. Order a bottle of Cristal so we can celebrate.

Order a bottle of expensive champagne? Yep, I can get on board with this. I haven't even met my date yet and I can already tell we're going to hit it off.

As I'm rereading the text, I see a waiter approach out of the corner of my eye. He addresses me with a polite, "Bon soir, Madame."

I order the champagne as I'm tucking my phone back into my purse, then look up at the waiter. He's handsome, with striking Nordic features that remind me of the male lead in a Scandinavian political thriller I binge watched last month.

As I'm studying him, the waiter's eyes widen a fraction, then a smile plays across his lips. "Is that you, Jasmine Cho?" he asks.

The man's English is flawless, yet there's a faint accent I can't quite place. Something about the vowels . . . wait a minute, how does this guy know my name?

I look at him more closely, then furrow my brow. "Asger Christensen?" I ask tentatively.

No, it can't be. The Asger I knew was a scrawny foreign exchange student who sat next to me in homeroom during the tenth grade. This guy is whatever the opposite of scrawny is. That waiter's jacket can't hide his broad shoulders, and I bet there are some serious muscles going on underneath that crisp white shirt.

I shake my head. Nope, this isn't that shy teenage boy I befriended on his first day at school in the States. Well, those blue eyes do look familiar . . .

He grins. "You look like a stunned mullet. It really is me, I swear."

I grin back. "How many times do I have to tell you that we don't use that expression in America? Besides, nobody likes to be compared to a fish."

"We're not in America," Asger points out. "This is Monaco."

"Yeah, I know." I chew on my bottom lip while I think about the odds of this chance encounter. "This is so weird running into you here. What are you doing here, anyway?"

"I could ask the same thing of you," he says before pulling me to my feet and embracing me.

I have a million questions I want to ask, but someone behind us clears their throat. As I step out of Asger's arms, I see the head waiter scowling at Asger before giving me one of those practiced smiles that doesn't quite reach the eyes.

Asger gives his boss an apologetic look before quickly explaining that we're old friends. The man purses his lips, then takes his leave, no doubt to make some other poor waiter's life miserable.

"I'll get you that champagne," Asger says to me.

"Hope I didn't get you in trouble," I say.

"Don't worry about it. He's a bit like old Mr. D."

As Asger heads over to the bar, I chuckle at the reminder of our old math teacher. If it hadn't been for Asger's help, I would have never passed that class.

A few minutes later, Asger returns with a bottle of Cristal in a champagne bucket and two glasses. As he places the glasses on the table, he says, "I assume you're meeting someone."

"Yes, my date," I say. "He should be here soon. We're celebrating a business deal he closed."

Asger holds up the champagne. "Do you want to wait until he arrives?"

I look at the bar's gilded clock, wondering how long my date will be. Surely, he wouldn't want me to sit here thirsty? "No, go ahead and pour me a glass. I have something to celebrate as well."

"Oh? What's that?" Asger asks as he uncorks the champagne.

"Running into you after all these years," I say with a smile. "What is it? Ten, twelve years?"

"Thirteen." Asger sets the glass in front of me. "It's an unlucky number in America, isn't it?"

"Ah, but we're in Europe," I remind him.

Asger sets the champagne bottle in the bucket. "How long are you in Monaco for?"

"A couple of months," I say.

His eyes light up. "Good. We'll have time to catch up."

A man at a neighboring table motions Asger over, so we quickly exchange cell phone numbers. As I watch Asger take the gentleman's order, I wonder what in the world he's doing waiting tables at a casino in Monaco. When I knew Asger in high school, he had a clear path laid out for him–return to Denmark after his exchange year, finish his studies, then go to work for his family's flat-pack furniture company.

There was definitely a story here that I wanted to know. But the problem with asking people about their stories was that they inevitably wanted to know yours in return. And I wasn't sure I was ready to tell Asger what had happened to me after he went back to Denmark.

* * *

As I sip my glass of Cristal, I think back to my high school days. The champagne bubbles tickle my nose, reminding me of the old-fashioned root beer floats my friends and I used to get after football games.

When I first introduced Asger to the concept of an ice cream float, he had been horrified. According to him, ice cream and soda were two separate items–one belonged in a bowl and the other in a glass. But after I cajoled him into trying a sip of my root beer float, he was sold.

"See, sometimes when you take two things you don't think go together and combine them, you end up with something amazing," I had said to him. "It's all about finding the perfect chemistry."

My phone buzzes, jolting me back to the present day. But instead of a text from my date saying he's on his way, it's a message from Asger with a cowboy emoji and a link to a country western music video. I'm curious what it's about, but I'll have to check it out later. Can you imagine the look on everyone's faces if I started playing a random country tune on my phone? Not exactly the type of music that goes with these elegant surroundings.

I'm starting to get irritated that my date still hasn't shown. I feel like people are staring at me and whispering things like, "Why's that girl sitting there on her own?" and "Is she going to drink that entire bottle herself?"

Spying a terrace off of the bar, I decide to slip outside and call my best friend. Olivia is usually so busy traveling around the world for work that I'm surprised when she answers the phone.

"You'll never guess who I just saw," I say. "Do you remember that foreign exchange student in tenth grade? The guy from Denmark?"

"Asger?" Olivia asks.

"That's the one," I say. "He's here in Monaco. I ran into him at the Monte Carlo Casino. I barely recognized him. Remember how scrawny he was? Well, not anymore. Muscles everywhere."

I smile inwardly, recalling the feel of Asger's strong arms as he hugged me, then add, "Remember how the kids in school used to tease Asger about his name? He explained that it comes from Old Norse and means 'the spear of God,' but that made it worse. I still cringe when I think about the nicknames some of the guys on the football team gave him."

"Uh-huh," Olivia says.

"Anyway, if they saw him now, they'd be in for a shock. Seriously, Asger has turned into a sexy Scandinavian god. If he had looked like that in high school, maybe I would have wanted to be more than friends."

"Hang on a sec. Did you say you're in Monaco?" Olivia asks. "Is your band on tour there?"

"How many times do I have to tell you that it's a string quartet, not a band." I chuckle, knowing Olivia is just trying to wind me up. "We're doing a private concert at some prince's birthday party. Hopefully, he's single."

"A second ago, you had your heart set on Asger," Olivia says.

I shake my head. "He's gorgeous to look at, but the man is a waiter. Anyway, enough about me. I'd ask you about your love life, but I'm sure it will be the same old story. 'I'm too busy with work to date, blah, blah, blah.'"

"Actually, I'm on vacation and I met a guy," Olivia says.

"No way. Where are you?" I ask.

"I'm on a beautiful Greek island with my aunt Celeste."

"Okay, we'll get back to the island in a minute. First, tell me about this guy." I lean over the railing and admire the lush gardens while Olivia tells me about how she's fallen for Xander, a Greek guy with a unibrow.

"Can you believe my aunt thinks love at first sight is a real thing?" she asks.

"She's right," I say. "You can fall for a guy in less than twenty minutes. Twenty-four hours later, you tell him you love him. Two days after that, you end up getting married."

Olivia is silent for a moment, then she says, "Why do I feel like you're not describing the plot of a Hallmark movie? Did you get married?"

"Kind of yes. But also no. It was annulled, so it's like it never happened." I take a deep breath, then let it out slowly. Olivia is my best friend, but this isn't really something I want to think about, let alone explain. I wave a waiter over and ask him to bring my glass of champagne from the table. "I don't really want to talk about it, if that's okay. Tell me more about your guy. You're obviously smitten with him."

"Smitten?" Olivia chuckles. "Listen to you. You sound like a character from one of those old movies that my aunt is always watching."

"Smitten is a great word. Don't mock it. Listen, your aunt is right. You definitely have feelings for this Xander. And from what you've said, he sounds pretty special. You know how I can tell?" I pause to grab the champagne glass from the waiter, then say, "All you could talk about was how he makes you laugh. Being able to have fun with someone is the secret to a long-lasting relationship. Of course, they have to have money as well."

"Not only are you a romantic, you're also a cynic," Olivia says.

"I'm realistic. Totally different thing. You said Xander owns lots of property on the island, and he used to be some high-powered corporate type. Sounds like he's loaded." I take a sip of my champagne, then say in a teasing tone, "I think you should quit your job and marry him."

After Olivia tells me how awful her boss is, I wonder if she might end up handing in her resignation after all. We chat for a few more minutes, then I end the call, telling her I need to freshen up before my date shows up. *If* he shows up. It's been nearly forty-five minutes already. I'm beginning to think I've been stood up.

Now more high school memories flood back, this

time less pleasant ones of my high school boyfriend Corey. We met during our freshman year and dated on and off until graduation. Whenever we had plans, Corey was either late or he didn't show up. He'd be super apologetic afterward, giving me a variety of excuses. Some were legitimate–football practice ran late or his car broke down. But the others were so flimsy that even Corey looked embarrassed telling them to me.

Did he really need to perform an emergency tracheotomy on his guinea pig? Was his little brother really abducted by aliens? I don't think so.

Although, come to think of it, I guess there was a reason why Corey got an 'A' in creative writing class. Last I heard, he was working as a spin doctor for a sleazy political candidate. Making up outlandish stories to excuse a politician's bad behavior? Sounds like Corey had found his calling.

After freshening up my makeup in the ladies' room, I head back into the bar and try to shake off the memories of how Corey had sweet-talked his way back into my good books time and time again. I remember Asger pointing out that a girl like me deserved better, but I had shrugged off his advice.

It feels like history is repeating itself. Here I am sitting at a table alone waiting for my date to show up while Asger shoots me sympathetic looks. Fortunately, my date sends a text assuring me he's on his way. When he tells me to order some caviar to go along with the Cristal, I smile. Is there anything better with champagne than caviar? I don't think so.

I wave Asger over. When I ask him to bring some caviar, he grins. "Fancy. I remember when your favorite snack was Pringles."

"I've grown up since then," I say.

My face grows warm when Asger locks his eyes with me and says softly, "I know."

It's a weird moment, full of a tension I can't quite put my finger on. I grab my phone and pull up my date's text so I can tell Asger what type of caviar he wanted me to order.

"How long have you two been seeing each other?" Asger asks, his tone a mix of politeness and skepticism.

"This will be our first date. A mutual acquaintance set us up." I toy with my bracelet. "I'm sure he'll be here soon."

Asger arches an eyebrow, then silently tops up my champagne before telling me he'll be right back with my order. But instead of Asger returning with the caviar, it's the cranky head waiter. He sets a crystal bowl of caviar nestled on a bed of crushed ice on the table along with a plate of dry toast points.

My mouth waters in anticipation as I scoop up some of the caviar with a mother-of-pearl spoon and place it on a piece of toast. As I bite down, the explosion of flavor is like none other–soft, fresh, buttery, nutty–there really aren't words to describe it adequately. But what I do know is that it is exquisite, like nothing else in the world.

After a second helping, I remind myself to leave some for my date. Then my phone buzzes, a sound I've come to dread. I steel myself for another text about how he'll be here shortly. But as I read his message, I feel like I'm going to be sick.

Sorry, can't make it after all. Enjoy your evening.

My stomach clenches as I look at the bottle of Cristal and the crystal bowl of caviar. How am I supposed to pay for this?

CHAPTER 2
WHISKEY AND BRAGI

When my alarm clock goes off the next morning, I want to fling it across the room. Since arriving in Monaco from the States a few days ago, I've been struggling with jet lag. My body can't seem to accept the fact that it's the crack of dawn here. It's still convinced I'm back in San Francisco ready to go to bed for the night. As much as I love all the international travel that comes with my job, the constant time changes play havoc on my sleep routine.

As I shuffle toward the bathroom, I realize that there's something else that impacted my quality of sleep last night. Not being able to stop thinking about being stood up at the casino had me tossing and turning for hours. I don't know what was worse–the embarrassment of my date not showing up or the fact that Asger had to bail me out when the check for the champagne and caviar arrived.

Taking a shower helps to wake me up. Once I dry off, I twist my long dark hair into a messy bun and apply a bit of makeup. Then I pull on some jeans and a t-shirt, slip on some sandals, and head downstairs to the kitchen for breakfast. As I skip down the marble staircase, I mentally pinch myself. How in the world did I end up staying at such a stunning villa in Monaco?

I know the answer, of course—Sebastien, the tall, red-haired cello player in our string quartet. Sebastian had grown up in Monaco, which meant that he came from money. Not only did he regularly hob-nob with the rich and famous, he even had royal connections, having dined more than once at the palace. Honestly though, the guy was so down to earth, you wouldn't know from speaking to him that his trust fund was larger than some countries' GDPs.

When one of Sebastien's friends—a minor European royal—asked if our quartet would play at his birthday party, Sebastien arranged to fly us to Monaco on his private plane and put us up at his family's villa. The plan was to use the villa as our base for the next couple of months while we prepared for our upcoming European tour, kicking off with the party. I could think of worse places to stay while we rehearsed.

"Look who's up." Grace, the other violinist in our quartet, glances up from the fruit she's chopping when I walk into the kitchen. Her green eyes sparkle with mischief as she tucks a lock of her curly blonde hair behind her ear. "I was about to send Pedro up to drag you out of bed."

"Two days in a row of Pedro, the human alarm clock, was enough for me." I shoot the Mexican viola player a look. "Do you really think yanking the curtains open and singing *La Cucaracha* at the top of your lungs is a pleasant way to start the day?"

"Buenos dias," Pedro says sweetly to me, his dark brown eyes crinkled with amusement. "Coffee?"

"Yes, please," I say, taking a seat next to Sebastien at the large marble kitchen island. "Extra strong."

Sebastien turns to me. "How did your date go?"

"Ugh." I put my head in my hands. "Not good. He never showed up. I looked like an idiot."

When I tell Sebastien the name of the guy who stood me up, he frowns and utters a few French swear words. "Oh, man, I wish I had known that's who you were going out with. He's such a douchebag."

"Been there, done that," Grace says as she places a skillet on the stove. "Being stood up is the worst."

Pedro sets an espresso in front of me, then gives Grace an incredulous look. "You've been stood up? No way. I can't imagine any guy not showing up for a date with you."

"But you can imagine it happening to me?" I ask

dryly.

"No, that's not what I meant. It's just that . . ." Pedro splutters.

"Don't worry. I know what you meant," I say, putting Pedro out of his misery.

Then Sebastien and I exchange a look. It's obvious to everyone but Grace that Pedro has a massive crush on her. But the last thing we need is for these two to hook up. Everything's fine when the romance is new, but as soon as the fighting starts, someone has to go. I've seen it happen in other groups. Grace, Sebastien, and I have played together for years, so Pedro would be the one who would have to leave. He's a sweet guy and a heck of a viola player, so it would be a huge loss.

I shake my head. Grace is oblivious to the puppy dog looks Pedro gives her. Nothing is going to happen between those two, I reassure myself.

"Grab the eggs from the fridge for me," Grace says to Pedro. "Then can you grate that gruyere cheese?"

While the two of them prepare breakfast, I sip my espresso and look at my phone. After deleting the texts from Mr. No Show, I glance at the link to the country music video Asger had sent me last night. Before I can check it out, Grace sets plates down in front of us. The sight of the cheese and mushroom omelet, fruit salad, and croissant makes my stomach grumble.

"Sorry, your evening turned out to be a disappointment," Sebastien says as I dig in.

"It wasn't all bad," I say in between bites. "I ran into an old friend from high school."

Grace takes a seat next to me. "What are the odds you'd run into someone from the States at the casino in Monaco. Is he one of those high-roller, jet-setter types you're so fond of?"

I chuckle. "No, he's a waiter at the casino."

Pedro shrugs. "There's nothing wrong with being a waiter."

"I totally agree with you," I say. "It's just not what I expected he'd end up doing."

"My parents wanted me to be a doctor," Grace says as she spreads jam on her croissant. "They were so disappointed when I told them I wanted to be a professional musician."

"I remember having the same conversation with my folks. Except not the doctor part," I quickly add. "The thought of blood freaks me out."

"So what did your parents want you to be?" Pedro asks.

"They always knew I wanted to do something with music, but I think they hoped I would have become a music teacher instead of trying to make a living playing professionally. It's not an easy business to break into."

"We do all right now," Grace says. "I mean, we're never going to get rich, but at least we can pay the bills."

"Yeah, but remember all those ramen years before

we got the quartet going?" I point out.

Grace smiles. "Don't forget the boxed macaroni and cheese."

I spear a piece of mango with my fork, then say, "Personally, I'd like to do better than just being able to pay the bills. I don't want to have to worry about money."

"Which is why you want to land a rich prince," Sebastien says as he wags a finger at me playfully.

"At least I'm honest about it," I say.

As Pedro gets up to grab another croissant, he asks Sebastien about the guy we're playing the private concert for. "Maybe you can set him up with Jasmine."

Sebastien gives a non-committal grunt. "I think she can do better."

"Tell us more about your high school friend," Grace says.

After sharing some stories about Asger's experiences as a foreign exchange student living in small town America, I mentioned how he had come to my rescue the previous night. "There I was staring at the check, wondering how I was going to pay it when Asger told me he'd take care of it."

"What do you mean he took care of it?" Grace asks.

"Well, I assume he comped the champagne and caviar," I say. "Like that guy did when we were in New York, remember?"

"You mean at the oyster bar?" Grace furrows her

brow. "Um, that guy owned the place. And he only gave us complimentary appetizers and drinks because he was hoping you'd give him your phone number. Which you didn't."

Pedro pipes up. "Didn't you say Asger is a waiter? I doubt he'd have the authority to write off such a big bill."

"Maybe his manager okayed it," Sebastien suggests.

Thinking back to the grumpy head waiter, I shake my head. Then my eyes widen as what they're saying sinks in. Did Asger pay for the champagne and caviar himself? He had always been such a good friend in high school, but to do this for me, thirteen years later, was too much. Way too much. How could I have been so insensitive? So stupid? So oblivious?

Feeling like a fool, I press my fingers to my eyes, fighting back tears. Sebastien squeezes my shoulder. "I'll give you the money to pay Asger back."

I start to protest, but Sebastien cuts me off. "Like I said, the guy that stood you up is a douchebag. Don't worry, I have an idea about how to make sure he pays me back."

"That sounds mysterious," Grace says.

Sebastien rubs his hands together. "The best ideas always are."

* * *

After we're finished with breakfast, I offer to clean up the kitchen while the others get ready for our morning rehearsal.

Normally, the villa is fully staffed with a live-in housekeeper and chef, but when the two of them fell head over heels in love and got married, Sebastien's family's wedding gift was an all-expense paid month-long honeymoon in the Caribbean. So we're responsible for cooking and tidying up after ourselves, which none of us mind.

Once the dishwasher is loaded and the counters wiped down, I make myself another espresso while I psych myself up to call Asger.

What was the best way to start the conversation? I pace back and forth for a few moments, then quickly dial before I lose my nerve. When Asger answers, I blurt out, "Sorry, I'm an idiot and I totally took advantage of your friendship but in my defense I didn't realize what I was doing and I've got a wad of cash for you that my friend gave me because he feels sorry that a douchebag stood me up."

There was silence on the other end, then Asger says, "Jasmine? Is that you? Did you butt dial me? Can you hear me? Okay, I'm going to hang up–"

I glare at my stupid phone. Ever since the last update, it randomly mutes itself. I quickly press the unmute button before Asger ends the call. "Don't hang up. I'm here."

But before I can repeat my lame apology, Asger

jumps in. "I'm glad you called. I was wondering what you thought about the music video."

"Oh, sorry, I haven't had a chance to look at it yet," I say. "We're about to start rehearsal, but I'll check it out after that."

"Promise me you will, okay? Your opinion is important to me."

"Um, sure," I say, wondering what's so important about this music video. "Listen, the reason I called is because–"

"Hang on a minute," Asger says. He has a muffled conversation with someone, then tells me he has to get going. "I'm not working tonight. Want to meet up for dinner? We have a lot to catch up on. Are you free?"

"Yes, but–"

"Perfect, I'll text you my address. Sorry, I've got to run. See you tonight," he says before signing off.

Great. Now I have to wait until this evening to apologize to Asger. It's going to eat away at me in the meantime.

As the anxiety bubbles up inside me, I finish my espresso, then go to join the others in the music room. Sebastian and Pedro are discussing the pizzicato passages in Debussy's String Quartet in G Minor, Grace is sitting at the grand piano playing scales, and a white Persian cat is stretched out in the dappled sunlight coming in through the large French windows.

I walk to the other end of the room to retrieve my instrument. Before opening my violin case, I set my phone on one of the occasional tables. Then I remember Asger's music video. The others are busy, so I perch on the edge of a velvet settee and press play.

The catchy tune has me tapping my toes and humming along. And that guy playing guitar, wow, is he ever good. Although that ridiculously large cowboy hat he's wearing is a bit over the top. Not only does it hide his face, it detracts from his performance.

Grace looks up from the piano. "What is that?"

Glancing back down at my phone, I say, "It's a band called 'Whiskey and Bragi.' Asger wanted me to check them out."

"Why?" Grace furrows her brow. "Doesn't he know you're a classical violinist?"

I roll my eyes. Grace is a bit of a musical snob. Despite having studied a variety of musical traditions while at conservatory, she can't wrap her head around why anyone would want to listen to anything other than classical music. Talk to her about pop music or rock and roll, and she's completely lost. For a while there, she thought Taylor Swift was a handbag designer. One of my favorite ways to annoy her is to play technopop music when we're in the car.

"He knows I played violin in high school. But we didn't get a chance to talk about what I do now," I tell Grace. "Asger was in the orchestra, too."

"What instrument did he play?" she asks.

"Harp." I frown as I remember how some of the students teased Asger for playing what was considered a girl's instrument. But he didn't care. They didn't have a harp at his school back in Denmark, so he was excited to get the chance to try something new during his foreign exchange year.

Grace looks satisfied with my response. She's always had a soft spot for harpists, considering them the unsung heroes of the orchestra. When I tell her that Asger also played guitar and drums in the show choir, she wrinkles her nose.

"Play it again," Pedro says. "The way the fiddle and bass harmonized together was interesting."

"I like the lyrics," Sebastien adds. "Especially the part about the cows sitting in the pews in church."

As both of the guys come sit next to me, Grace shrugs and leafs through some sheet music. Pedro grabs my phone and turns up the volume and we listen to the song a couple more times.

"Maybe we should get costumes like they're wearing," Sebastien jokes. "You girls are always in black dresses, us guys are always in black suits. It's so boring. Sequined cowboy hats might liven up our performances."

Curiosity has gotten the better of Grace because she's now perched on the armrest of the couch. She nudges Pedro. "Let me see."

While Grace checks out the music video, Sebastien

reminds us of the schedule over the next couple of months. He looks pointedly at Pedro, who has a tendency to forget where he's supposed to be and when. "Maybe you want to write this down."

Pedro taps the side of his head. "It's all up here."

"Really?" Sebastien folds his arms across his chest. "Why don't you do a little recap for us."

"Sure, we have the prince's birthday party next Saturday–"

Sebastien cuts Pedro off. "Not next Saturday, *this* Saturday."

"Hey, at least I got the day of the week right." Pedro gives Sebastien a cocky grin. "Then after that, you're leaving us on our lonesome for a couple of weeks while you go superyacht shopping."

"I'm only going to be gone for a week. I have some meetings in New York for my family's business." At first, Sebastien looks like he wants to throttle Pedro, then a smile creeps across his face. "Besides, I already own a superyacht."

The Persian cat pads over to where we're sitting and sprawls on the carpet in front of Pedro. As he reaches down to stroke the cat's belly, Pedro casually says, "Jasmine, I don't know why you're looking for a millionaire to hook up with when you've got Mr. Superyacht right here. He probably has a helicopter, too."

"She's not exactly my type. I don't mean that in a bad way. I'm not her type either. Jasmine and I have talked about it before," Sebastien says to Pedro, then he squeezes my hand. "But any other guy would be lucky to have someone like Jasmine in their life."

"Aww, that's so sweet," I say, leaning in as he puts his arm around me.

"Seriously though, you should set your sights on someone who treats you well and who loves music as much as you do," Sebastien says to me. "A lot of rich guys are jerks. They treat women as a possession, not as a partner. That's not what you want, is it?"

"Of course not." I scoot back so I can look Sebastien in the eye. "But I've also seen firsthand how money worries can tear a couple apart. When my parents had to declare bankruptcy, the stress of it nearly drove them to divorce. There are millionaires out there who are decent human beings. Why not marry one of them instead of a guy who's broke?"

"Just be careful with your heart, okay?" Sebastien says.

I press my lips together. "After what happened earlier this year with that con artist, you better believe I am."

Pedro looks up from petting the cat. "What con artist?"

"It happened before you joined the quartet," Sebastien says.

"I'd rather not talk about it, if you don't mind," I say to Pedro. "Grace and Sebastien are probably tired of hearing about it. Isn't that right, Grace?"

"Huh?" Grace says, her eyes glued to my phone.

"Nothing," I say. "What are you looking at anyway that has you so engrossed?"

"I was checking out that band's website." She makes a lassoing motion with her hand. "Yee-haw!"

"See, country music is cool," Pedro says.

I shake my head. "She's being sarcastic."

Grace grins at me. "The only redeeming thing about this group is their guitar player. He's cute. Blond hair, blue eyes . . . exactly your type."

"Let me see." I grab the phone from Grace, then do a double take when I see the picture of Whiskey and Bragi's homepage. "Oh, my gosh, that's Asger."

CHAPTER 3
DATE DRESS

Later that night, I walk into the kitchen to let the others know I'm heading out. Pedro is helping Grace make pasta carbonara while Sebastien opens a bottle of wine. I smile when the Persian cat knocks the cork off the counter.

Sebastien shoos the cat away as he sets the corkscrew down. Then he gives me an appreciative whistle. "Your date is a lucky guy."

"It's not a date," I say. "Just two old high school friends catching up."

Sebastien shakes his head. "Not in that dress. That's a date dress."

I look over at Grace to get her opinion. "What do you think?"

She cracks some eggs into a bowl, then says, "It

could go either way. It's a casual sundress and you aren't showing a lot of cleavage, but the off the shoulder straps have a kind of a, um . . ."

"Sexy vibe," Sebastien says, finishing her sentence.

Pedro pipes up. "You're wearing a new eyeshadow, aren't you?"

"You people need to get a life," I say. As I flounce out of the kitchen, I yell over my shoulder, "It's not a date."

When I get outside, I debate whether to take a taxi or go on foot. Based on the map on my phone, Asger's place is only a mile and a half away. I'm wearing ballet flats, the weather is gorgeous, and I've been cooped up inside all day rehearsing. A walk it is.

As I stroll through the streets of Monaco, I smile to myself. Who would have thought Asger would end up in a country band? Once I realized that he was the one playing guitar and singing in the music video, I scoured the internet for more information.

Apparently, Asger had founded Whiskey and Bragi two years ago, shortly after he moved from Denmark to Monte Carlo. Whiskey was a reference to his childhood dog, a red-golden Danish Mastiff. Bragi came from the Norse god of poetry and music.

There was an image of a 19th century painting of Bragi on the band's site, showing the god holding a harp while his wife, the goddess Iðun, stands next to him. Someone with a sense of whimsy had superimposed cowboy hats on Bragi and Iðun's heads.

The whole thing summed up what I had known about Asger in high school–a mix of scholarly intellect and a hilarious sense of humor.

I'm so lost in thought that I nearly trip over a curb. I pause at the corner of an intersection to check to make sure I'm headed in the right direction. According to the map, once I cross this street, I'll be in France where Asger lives. Can you believe it? It seems crazy to me that you can walk from one country to another and not even realize it.

Sebastien had told me that most people who work in Monaco can't afford to live in the principality, so they commute each day from the neighboring country. That would be Asger's situation. A waiter's salary can only stretch so far, and, from what I can tell, Whiskey and Bragi is like a million other bands out there–a bunch of struggling musicians hoping to make it big.

When I reach Asger's street, I pause to catch my breath. If I had realized how steep the roads in this area were, I might have opted for a taxi. I take in my surroundings. The buildings that line the street are far more modest than Sebastien's villa, but the yellow stucco walls covered in bougainvillea, wrought-iron balconies, and white shutters are charming. I sure didn't see anything like this growing up in my small town.

I don't need to look around for Asger's address. A converted garage with country music blaring from it–

that's got to be it. No surprise that no one hears me knocking. I push open the door and grin at the sight of Asger wearing a Dolly Parton t-shirt underneath a brown leather vest with fringe.

Asger's biceps flex as he picks the strings on his guitar. The bluegrass melody is haunting, the series of notes speaking to the sort of pain that sticks with us no matter how much we try to shake it. I'm already in awe of Asger's talent but when he begins singing, shivers go down my spine. His gravelly voice wraps around each word, the emotional undercurrents of each lyric drawing me in.

I barely notice when the other band members join in. The beat of the drums and the low, steady pulse of the bass guitar add to the overall effect, but my attention is squarely on Asger. Not only is he a superb musician, he exudes a charisma that makes me realize this guy could be a star.

When the last plaintive notes of the song die out, I start clapping. Asger looks over at me, registering surprise that I'm standing there. Then a smile creeps across his face. "When did you get here?"

"Not soon enough," I say. "That was amazing. I wish I had heard the whole song."

Asger sets his guitar down, then walks over and kisses me on the cheek. The feeling of his lips brushing against my skin makes me feel uncomfortable. Not because it doesn't feel good, but because it feels too good. I can feel my heart pounding as Asger goes to kiss my other cheek in the way that Europeans do. Thankfully, he doesn't linger, stepping back to introduce me to the other members of the band.

"Come meet the guys." Asger puts his arm around the bass guitar player, a large man with dreadlocks and glasses with purple frames. "This is Jean-Baptiste. We call him J.B. for short."

J.B. grins at me. "Pleasure to meet you, Jasmine. Asger hasn't been able to shut up about you since yesterday."

I smile when Asger shoots him a look, then I ask J.B. if he's American. "Until I heard your accent, I assumed with a name like Jean-Baptiste you were French or Monegas . . . Monegas. . ."

As my tongue trips over the word for someone from Monaco, Asger comes to the rescue. "Monégasque," Asger says slowly so I can hear each syllable. Then he tells me that there aren't actually that many Monégasques. "Less than forty thousand people live in the principality, and only around a quarter of those are Monaco nationals. It's a pretty exclusive club."

"You're just full of facts, aren't you?" I tease him. "Probably why you got straight As in high school."

Asger waves away my comment and points at a man with long sandy-brown hair tied back in a ponytail. "This is our drummer, Raphael. He's a French citizen. I met him working at the casino."

As Raphael and I shake hands, I ask if he's also a waiter.

"No, I'm a croupier," he says. When I furrow my brow, he explains. "I manage the roulette wheel."

"I've always wanted to play roulette, like in one of those James Bond movies," I say.

"You wouldn't be the first," Raphael says with a smile. "Come by the casino sometime and I'll teach you."

"That's probably not a good idea. I think you should only gamble if you can afford to lose your money." As the words leave my mouth, I remember the money I have in my purse to repay Asger. Sebastien seemed so at ease handing me the sizable sum earlier in the day, like it was pocket change to him. I felt less comfortable accepting his generosity.

"We have another band member, but she got a call and disappeared." Asger presses his lips together, then adds, "Terese plays the fiddle like you do."

"I play the violin, not the fiddle," I point out.

"It's the same instrument. Only the music you play on it is different," Asger says playfully. "It's all a matter of–"

Raphael shushes Asger as a woman in her early twenties rushes into the room. Mascara and eyeliner are smudged around her eyes in a way that could either be a trendy new look or the result of her crying. Based on the way she's sniffling, I think it's the latter.

"Everything okay?" Asger asks her.

"No," she says curtly as she grabs her backpack off a chair and slings it over her shoulder.

"Hey, what's going on?" Raphael asks the woman.

She responds in French, gesticulating wildly with her hands while pacing back and forth. I struggle to follow the rapid-fire conversation, but the gist of it seems to have to do with her deadbeat boyfriend. Raphael seems to be reassuring her that everything will be okay, but she stamps her feet, then storms out, slamming the door behind her.

J.B. looks back and forth at Raphael and Asger. "What just happened?"

Asger sinks onto a tattered couch in the corner and puts his head in his hands. "Terese is threatening to quit the band."

Knowing the havoc it causes when you have to replace a member of a musical group, I feel for Asger. When I tell him how sorry I am, Asger shrugs. Then he starts to laugh, but his laughter has an edge to it. As Raphael goes to sit next to Asger, I give J.B. a questioning look.

Before J.B. can explain, Asger says bitterly. "This is what happens when you think you're about to get your big break. The gods decide to mess with you."

"What big break?" I ask.

"It doesn't matter." Asger shakes his head. "Without Terese, it's not going to happen."

"I'll try talking to her," J.B. says. Then his eyes

light up. "But if I'm not successful, maybe Jasmine could–"

Asger cuts him off. "No, let's not go there. She wouldn't be interested."

"Interested in what?" I ask.

But Asger avoids answering, instead saying that we should get going and head out to dinner. As I wait for him to pack away his guitar, I'm left with two questions. What's this mysterious big break of his? And what does he think I wouldn't be interested in?

* * *

As we step outside, Asger offers his arm to me and I slip my hand through it like it's the most natural thing in the world. There's a light breeze now, wafting the light citrusy scent of the flowering bougainvillea in our path. I feel like I'm in an exquisite perfume shop, not walking on a sidewalk next to a busy road.

When we cross the invisible border between France and Monaco, I stop in the middle of the intersection and take a photo with my phone.

"There's more interesting things than a crosswalk to take pictures of," Asger says.

"Not to me." I hop over to one side of the road and say, "France." Then I hop back, saying "Monaco." I repeat this a few times until the driver of a Mercedes Benz impatiently honks his horn. Asger tugs my arm and pulls me onto the sidewalk on the Monégasque side.

"You're goofy," he says.

I stick my tongue out. "Takes one to know one."

We both break into laughter, collapsing into each other's arms. When we get control of ourselves, I say, "I didn't realize how much I missed you until now."

Asger puts his hands on my shoulders and locks his eyes with me. "Same."

That same uncomfortable feeling comes over me. Goosebumps, a fluttering heart. Nope, this is not what's supposed to happen when you're hanging out with an old high school buddy.

I pull back slightly, then ask, "So, where are we going for dinner?"

Asger drops his hands and points down the road. "There's a place a couple of blocks away from here. Nothing fancy, but it's good. You like pasta?"

"Who doesn't like pasta?" The breeze picks up, blowing my hair into my eyes. As I tuck it back behind my ears, I say, "Do they only serve Italian food? I was hoping to try a Monégasque dish. Although, now that I think about it, nothing comes to mind. Do they have their own distinct cuisine? Or is it mostly French?"

"There's an appetizer called barbagiuan," Asger explains. "It's a kind of fritter that's stuffed with Swiss chard, rice, and ricotta."

I smile. "Swiss chard, huh? Wouldn't that make it Swiss, not Monégasque?"

"What do they call those things they serve at McDonald's again?" Asger taps his finger to his lips in a mocking gesture. "Oh, yeah. French fries. You guys seem to think they're as American as apple pie despite the name."

"Hah-hah." I nudge Asger with my elbow. "Come on, I'm getting hungry for some of this Monégasque-Swiss fritter."

When we reach the restaurant, Asger holds open the door. I'm immediately greeted by the smell of something garlicky. "Whatever that is, I'll have it," I say as my mouth waters.

Asger orders the barbagiuan for both of us to start with, then suggests that I try the house specialty as my main course–Spaghetti alla Nerano.

"Does it have garlic in it?" I ask the waiter. When he nods, I don't ask any more questions. A dish with pasta and garlic. That's all I need to know.

While Asger orders a carafe of the house wine to go with our meal, I look around the establishment. It's small and homey, a far cry from the expensive-looking restaurants I've seen in other parts of Monte Carlo. The red-checkered tablecloths and lace curtains are a little tattered, the tiled floor has chips in a few places, and the wood chairs are mismatched. But everything is clean and gives the appearance of being well-loved. And, clearly, the food must be fantastic because the place is packed.

Asger looks at home here, waving hello to some of

the patrons and joking around with the waiter. It must be nice to have some place where you feel like you belong. Being on the road touring with the Fjura Quartet means I'm not in one place for very long. It'll be a real treat to spend the next couple of months in Monaco. Especially if it means I can spend time renewing my friendship with Asger.

Friendship. I repeat that word in my mind a few times. Friends is all we are, and friends is all I want us to be. Despite how my body tingles when Asger kisses my cheek or puts his hands on my shoulders, I know he's not right for me. Yes, this restaurant is cute and I'm sure the pasta is to die for, but this isn't the type of place I see myself going to with my future husband. I'm a champagne and caviar kind of girl. I know it's shallow, but it's what I want from life. End of story.

As the waiter pours wine into our glasses, I study Asger. I wonder if there's such a thing as a Viking cowboy. His white-blond hair, deep-set blue eyes, high cheekbones and tall build speaks to his Scandinavian heritage, but his Dolly Parton t-shirt is all country. Thankfully, he swapped out his leather fringe vest for a denim jacket before we left his place. It raises fewer eyebrows.

"So, what do you think of the barbagiuan?" Asger asks.

"It's delicious," I say between bites. "I've never really been a fan of Swiss chard, but now I think I'm a convert."

"How do you feel about dried cod?" Asger asks.

I finish the last morsel of my appetizer, then set my utensils down. "I'm not sure I've ever had it."

"Well, that needs to change. Next time we go for dinner, we'll get some stocafi. It's another traditional Monégasque dish made with dried cod."

As the waiter clears our plates, I tell Asger that I'm paying for tonight's meal.

"No, I invited you to dinner," he says. "I'm paying."

"Nope, it's on me. After you helped me out last night when my date stuck me with the check, I owe you." I reach into my purse and pull out the envelope of cash Sebastien gave me. "And speaking of that, here's the money to cover the champagne and caviar. I'm embarrassed to admit that I didn't think about the fact that you paid the check for me. I was upset about being ditched, but that's no excuse."

"I, um, I didn't . . ." Asger's face flushes, and I reach out and squeeze his hand.

"Yes, you did. It was sweet, but you shouldn't have." I push the envelope toward Asger, then add, "Besides, on a waiter's salary, you can't afford that kind of thing."

"How do you know I'm not a trust fund baby?" he asks.

I cock my head to one side. "Are you?"

After a beat, Asger frowns. "No, thank goodness. I plan on making my own way in the world."

Asger continues to put up a fight, but I keep insisting until he finally tucks the money into the pocket of his jacket. Then he smiles at me. "But tonight's dinner is my treat, no ifs, ands, or buts. Okay?"

I hold up my hands in surrender. "Fine."

While the waiter sets our plates of Spaghetti alla Nerano on the table, I mentally check "Pay Back Asger" off my to-do list, then write down "Pay Back Sebastien" and "No More Blind Dates" underneath.

The pasta dish is amazing–fried zucchini slices, fresh basil, grated Parmesan-Reggiano, and lots of garlic. It pairs perfectly with the crisp white wine. Neither of us speaks for several minutes, concentrating on our food instead. Once we come up for air, we get caught up on what has gone on in our lives over the past thirteen years.

Not that you can really condense over a decade of experience into a couple of hours, but we hit the highlights. Or at least the highlights that we chose to share with each other. I'm sure Asger kept some things from me. I know I did from him.

My story was pretty simple. After graduating college, I went on to get my masters at the San Francisco Conservatory of Music, which is where I met Grace. After my studies were finished, I scraped by, playing in a local chamber orchestra, teaching private violin lessons, and picking up other gigs when I could. My work and social life revolved around the classical music scene.

Grace and I had befriended Sebastien when he moved to the Bay Area, and when he suggested forming a string quartet with another musician we knew, both of us jumped at the chance. Touring around the world with good friends and playing music. Yes, please, sign me up.

Asger's life had taken a different path. After his foreign exchange year in the States, he returned to Denmark, did another year of secondary schooling before attending the University of Copenhagen. Once he got his degree, he went to work for his family's business.

"Honestly, I never thought I had a future that didn't involve flat-pack furniture," Asger says after taking a sip of his wine.

I lean forward. "I have a bone to pick with you. How come the instructions that come with flat-pack furniture are impossible to follow? And why are there never enough screws?"

Asger laughs so hard that he nearly snorts his wine out of his nose. "I think you're referring to the type of furniture you get at a certain Swedish store that also sells meatballs. My family crafts premium, high-end *Danish* flat-pack furniture. Completely different. In fact, we don't expect our clients to assemble their furniture themselves. We send someone to do that for them."

"Um, then, what's the point?" I furrow my brow.

"Flat-pack furniture is for people who can't afford furniture that already comes assembled."

"Not true. There are lots of rich folks who are flat-pack fanatics. My family business has a bit of a cult following."

"Wow, I had no idea people were so crazy for furniture that has to be put together," I say. Then I ask the question that's been burning in my mind. "How did you end up working at the casino and playing in a country band in Monaco?"

Asger holds up his wine glass. "I think we might need something stronger than this before I tell you that story."

CHAPTER 4
ZOOM ZOOM

Asger's idea of something stronger to drink is a coffee at a café situated on the pier at the Port de Fontvieille. The breeze has kicked up, so Asger insists that I wear his denim jacket. Then he suggests taking a taxi to the café. When I tell him I'm fine walking, Asger glances at my feet and smiles. "I like a girl who wears comfortable shoes."

I snort. "So, ladies who wear orthopedic shoes are your thing?"

"Yeah, I love a woman with bunions." Asger tries to keep a straight face, but fails. "Super sexy."

"I'll have you know these are designer shoes," I say, looking down at my ballet flats.

Asger grins. "Only the best for your bunions."

"Okay, enough weird foot talk." I loop my arm

through Asger's, cocking my head in the direction of the café. "Let's go get that coffee."

We stroll in a comfortable silence that reminds me of our high school study sessions. Back then, I was aware of Asger sitting in the chair next to me at the library, but it wasn't distracting. I could focus on my textbooks, happy to be in the company of my friend.

Now, as we walk through the streets of Monte Carlo, I'm hyperaware of Asger. My hand tingles as it brushes against his bicep. I want to snake my fingers underneath the sleeve of his Dolly Parton t-shirt and explore more of his muscular build. Chewing on my bottom lip, I fight the compulsion to touch him that way.

I sense Asger watching me as we walk past the superyachts moored along the Quay Jean-Charles Rey. Releasing my hand from his arm, I point at a sign which says 'Café de Formula 1' on the next block. "Is that where we're going?"

He nods. "Are you a fan of race car driving?"

"I can't say I know much about it other than the fact that they go zoom zoom around a track."

"There's a little more to it than 'zoom zoom,' especially when it comes to Formula 1." Asger pauses outside the café and points behind us. "You just missed the Monaco Grand Prix. It's one of the most prestigious automobile races in the world. The course runs along the water toward the casino and back, winding through the city streets."

"Sounds scary." I try to picture the race cars tearing through the narrow city streets. "How fast do they go?"

"This is one of the slower courses," Asger explains. "The top speed is only around hundred and eighty miles per hour."

My eyes widen at the prospect of cars going that fast. "Do you know, I don't even own a car. In fact, I can't even remember the last time I've been in the driver's seat. Years maybe."

Asger chuckles as he ushers me inside the café. "Remind me not to be in the passenger seat next time you get behind the wheel."

We find a secluded table next to a display case of racing memorabilia. The waiter raises his eyebrow when I order a latte. I know it's not the done thing in many parts of Europe to have a milky coffee drink except in the morning, but what the heart wants, the heart wants. And right now it wants coffee with all the milk.

My heart beats a little faster as Asger orders an espresso. I think it's trying to tell me that it wants something else, like the sexy Scandinavian guy sitting across from me. But we're not going there. Nope. No way. This heart of mine is going to have to be satisfied with a rush from the caffeine in my latte, not from running my fingers through Asger's hair or brushing my thumb across his lower lip.

Fortunately, Asger mistakes my air of distraction

for a fascination with the café's decor. As he points out a photo of the most recent winner of the Monaco Grand Prix, I try to get my emotions under control. When the waiter arrives with our drinks, I take the opportunity to shift the conversation from motorsports to how Asger ended up moving from Denmark to living near the Mediterranean Sea.

Asger looks down at his coffee cup. "There was this girl. I met her at a concert in Copenhagen. Then I stupidly followed her to Monaco."

When he doesn't elaborate, I gently ask. "Is there still a girl?"

"No, it didn't work out." Asger toys with a sugar packet for a moment before tearing it open. As he dumps the contents into his cup, he says, "She decided to go to Thailand, and, um . . . well, I stayed here."

"I'm sorry," I say. "Break-ups are hard."

There's a long silence as Asger sips his coffee. I want to ask him for more details. What was her name? How long did you date? How serious were things? Were you in love with her? But the haunted look in his eyes makes me hesitate.

When Asger does finally speak, it's to ask about my love life. Ugh. Dwelling on my past relationships is something I don't want to do, especially the last one. That one ended in an impromptu wedding. The annulment that quickly followed erased the marriage legally, but not from my memory. The whole episode was so cringe-worthy.

I take a deep breath, then let it out slowly. Trying to strike a light tone, I say, "You know how my last date went. Mr. No Show."

"That's what Corey used to do to you in high school," Asger says. "I never understood why you put up with how he treated you. You deserved so much better."

"At least now I'm in my champagne and caviar era when I get stood up," I joke. "Beats my soft drink and fries era in high school."

"Maybe it's time for a new era," Asger suggests.

"Maybe." I shrug. "What's your current era?"

"I'm not sure. I think I might be looking for a new one, too," Asger says thoughtfully. Then he leans forward. "You're not the only one who's been stood up, you know."

I furrow my brow. "Really?"

"Uh-huh. By that girl I was telling you about." Asger points at a table in the far corner of the café. "Actually, it happened right over there. We had arranged to meet after work, and she never showed. I waited for over an hour. I got worried when she didn't respond to any of my texts. Then, when I got back to our apartment, there was a note saying she was leaving me—"

I hold up a hand. "Hang on a minute. You were living together?"

Asger nods. "We had been dating for about six

months. Things were starting to get serious, so we decided to get a place together and see where things took us. We moved into our new apartment exactly two weeks before she ditched me."

"Wow. That's rough."

Asger leans back in his chair and looks up at the ceiling. "We had talked about going to Thailand together. Apparently, 'together' meant something different to her."

"How long since the two of you broke up?" On the surface, my question seems innocent, but I'm well aware that what I really want to know is if Asger is over his ex yet.

"About a year and a half." Asger finishes his espresso, then says, "Despite what happened at the end, I'm grateful to her for one thing."

"Oh, yeah? What's that?"

"She convinced me to form Whiskey and Bragi. While she might not have believed in us as a couple, she believed in my music." Asger sighs. "I hope J.B. was able to talk Terese into staying with the band. If not, we're screwed."

"It can't be that bad," I say. "There are worse things, right?"

"Compared to world hunger and living in war zones, you're right. But this is my one big chance. Opportunities like this don't come around every day." Asger picks his phone up from the table. "Hang on a sec, J.B. just texted. He wants me to call him."

While Asger is outside the café talking to his bandmate, I get a text of my own from Mr. No Show, wondering if I'm free for a champagne brunch tomorrow at a restaurant I've been dying to go to. For a nanosecond, I hesitate, but then I come to my senses and send the text directly to spam and block his number. Asger is right–I deserve better.

* * *

When Asger comes back into the café, his shoulders are slumped and the expression on his face is grim.

"I take it J.B. couldn't talk Terese into staying in the band," I say to Asger as he sits down.

"It's a lost cause." Asger shakes his head. "J.B. is the type of guy who can charm the shell off a turtle, but not this time."

"I wonder what turtles look like without their shells," I muse. "What are they hiding inside of them? Maybe turtle shells are like a woman's purse. They keep their change and lipstick inside. Or maybe turtles are really androids and that's how they conceal their true nature from us humans."

This makes Asger smile. "There's a turtle exhibit at the Oceanographic Museum in Monaco. Why don't we go check it out and get the answers to all your burning questions?"

"It's a date." When Asger raises an eyebrow, I quickly add, "Not a date-date, more like a, um . . ."

"Friend-date?" Asger suggests. "Two friends making plans to go somewhere together, right?"

"Exactly," I say, feeling both relieved and disappointed that we're on the same page. I quickly change the subject. "I remember you being a big Tim McGraw and Carrie Underwood fan in high school, but I would never have guessed you would end up in a country music band."

"Don't forget Kenny Rogers and Johnny Cash," Asger says. "They were my original idols."

I point at Asger's t-shirt. "What about Dolly?"

"She came later," he admits. "One of these days, I want to go back to the States and visit Dollywood. That's one of the things I would have done with the prize money."

"You lost me. What prize money?"

Asger orders another espresso, then fills me in on the competition due to take place in Monte Carlo at the end of the month. "It's called the Riviera Musical Rodeo," he explains. "It's a new event being bankrolled by this prince who wants to make Monte Carlo the Nashville of Europe. There are three big prizes up for grab–best original song, best band, and best singer. The winners get a big check and a recording contract."

I furrow my brow. "I didn't think country music was that popular on this side of the Atlantic."

"You'd be surprised. More and more people are listening to it. Everyone is hoping that the Riviera

Musical Rodeo puts country music firmly on the map here. They've been doing a lot of publicity about it." Asger leans forward, warming to his subject. "Over five hundred bands from around the world sent in audition videos. Only ten were selected to compete at the event. Whiskey and Bragi was one of them."

When I congratulate Asger on getting through to the in-person event, he frowns. "Yeah, we were pretty excited. Having to withdraw sucks. We thought we had a real shot."

"I know there isn't much time between now and when the competition takes place, but is there any chance you can find someone to take Terese's place?" Realizing that the odds of finding a fiddle player who can jump in at the last minute and get up to speed are slim, I answer my own question. "I guess not."

As Asger stares off blankly in the distance, it dawns on me what J.B. meant before. "What about me?"

Asger swivels his head in my direction and gives me a confused look. "What about you?"

"Why don't I fill in for Terese?"

He chuckles. "You don't play the fiddle."

"You said it yourself earlier. The instrument is the same, it's just the music you play on it that's different. I'm sure Joshua wouldn't mind."

Asger's jaw tightens. "Joshua?"

"Joshua Bell," I say innocently. "The guy I go to bed with each night and wake up with each morning."

"Sorry, I didn't realize you had a boyfriend," Asger

says after a beat. "You should have invited him to join us for dinner."

"Actually, he's not a very good dining companion. He just sits there woodenly without saying a word."

"I see." Asger clears his throat. "We should get the check. Joshua will be wondering where you are."

I suppress a smile as he waves the waiter over. I had forgotten how much fun it is to tease Asger. The waiter approaches and I quickly hand him my card before Asger can protest. As I'm tucking the receipt into my purse, Asger gives me a puzzled look.

"If you already have a boyfriend, why were you on a blind date last night?" He smacks his forehead. "Oh, I get it. Joshua Bell isn't a real person."

"Bite your tongue," I say. "Joshua Bell is very real. Only the best violinist of our time."

Asger holds up his hands. "Okay, I'm really confused."

Taking pity on him, I say, "I named my violin after him."

"Right, I get it." Asger chuckles. "He's wooden and not a good dining companion."

I smile. "And he sleeps in my room each night."

"It's getting late." Asger smiles back at me. "We should get you back to Joshua."

As Asger gets up from the table, I tell him that I was serious about my offer. "Obviously, I have to talk to the other members of the quartet, but if we can work out the rehearsal schedule, I'm sure they'd be okay with me filling in for Terese."

Asger shakes his head. "I appreciate the offer, I really do, but it's not going to work."

"I'm a quick study," I say.

"I know you are." Asger puts his hand on the small of my back and guides me toward the door. "But still, it's a lot."

"Couldn't you rearrange some of the songs to make the fiddle parts easier?"

As we walk outside, Asger tells me that the original song he's written is designed to showcase the fiddle. "It wouldn't be the same if I rearranged it."

"But what if–"

Asger puts his finger on my lips. "Even if you were able to learn the songs we're playing, there's one other major problem. The rules are very clear–we can't substitute musicians."

I think back to my brief encounter with Terese. We're both about the same height and build, we both have dark hair and eyes, and our features are similar. If you didn't know us well, you might think we were sisters. Okay, you might have to squint to see the resemblance, but with a giant cowboy hat hiding my face, I think I can pull this off.

Asger looks at me in confusion when I grab his hand and shake it. "Hi, nice to meet you. My name is Terese and I play fiddle for Whiskey and Bragi."

CHAPTER 5
PRINCE CHARMING

"You did what?" Grace asks me the next morning. We're in Sebastien's kitchen preparing breakfast. Eggs were on the menu, but Grace dropped them on the floor when I told her about my plan to fill in for Terese at the Riviera Musical Rodeo.

As I bend down to wipe up the eggy mess, Grace stares at me, her eyes wide with shock. After the floor is clean, I explain what transpired the previous night with Asger. When I'm finished, Grace grins at me. "You've got it bad."

"What do you mean?" I ask as I wash my hands.

"You've got it bad for Asger," she clarifies.

"No, I don't." I grab a dish towel. "We're friends. I'm helping my friend. That's all."

"Uh-huh."

I dry my hands then fling the dish towel on the counter. "You're making this out to be a bigger deal than it is."

"Sure."

"You know I'm not interested in Asger romantically." I stomp over to the fridge and get a container of orange juice out.

"You don't say."

Before I can refute her ridiculous insinuations, Sebastien and Pedro walk into the kitchen. Pedro gets to work pulling dishes and glasses out of the cupboards, while Sebastien asks Grace if she's making omelets again for breakfast.

"No, sorry," she says. "We're out of eggs."

Sebastien furrows his brow. "But there were plenty yesterday."

"Grace dropped them," I say in a teasing tone.

She arches an eyebrow. "And whose fault is that?"

I put a hand to my chest. "I wasn't holding them."

"Maybe if you hadn't shocked me with your news, we'd still have eggs," she says.

When the guys give me a questioning look, Grace tells them to take a seat. "Why don't I make some oatmeal and bacon while Jasmine fills you in on her crazy plan?"

Sebastien pours coffee for himself and Pedro, then both of them take their places on stools at the kitchen island. While Grace grates some apples to add to the oatmeal, I tell the guys how Terese quit Whiskey and Bragi.

"Asger told me that Terese's boyfriend has been putting a lot of pressure on her to spend more time with him," I say. "Apparently, he's jealous that she rehearses with the band in her free time. He's been wanting her to quit playing the fiddle for a while."

"Doesn't he realize that music is what makes her who she is?" Pedro shakes his head. "You can't tell a musician not to play their instrument, or an artist to stop painting, or a writer to stop writing. It would be like cutting off their arm. If you take away their creative outlet, they wouldn't be a whole person anymore."

Grace looks up from the cutting board. "Very well said."

As Pedro basks in Grace's approval, Sebastien asks what Terese has to do with me.

"There's a big country music competition taking place at the end of the month," I say. "Whiskey and Bragi is one of twenty bands selected to take part. It's really important to Asger. If they win, they get a cash prize and a recording contract. It's the big break he's been hoping for."

"Ah, I see. He wants you to fill in for Terese." Sebastien takes a sip of his coffee, then looks at Grace. "You're worried about how Jasmine is going to learn the fiddle parts in time?"

She shakes her head. "No, that's not it."

"So it's the scheduling issues that are bothering you." Sebastien pulls up the calendar on his phone. "Well, let's work through it. The prince's birthday party is on Saturday. That's the day after tomorrow. Rehearsal went well yesterday. If we focus on the Shostakovich piece today, then I think we'll be in good shape."

Grace starts to say something, but the microwave beeps. As she pulls the bacon out and flips it over, Sebastien continues to talk through our plans. "I leave on Sunday for New York for a week. We weren't planning on rehearsing while I'm gone, so Jasmine is completely free."

"When is the competition?" Pedro asks.

"It's in a couple of weeks," I say. "It starts with the preliminary round on the Saturday. Then the top three bands in each category go on to the final round one week after that."

Sebastien looks at me thoughtfully. "So that's when things get tricky. We have a recital on Sunday after the competition is over. Once I'm back from New York, we need to rehearse that week to make sure we're ready."

"Agreed," I say. "But we usually rehearse during the day. Asger and his band's rehearsals are scheduled for the night."

Grace scoops out oatmeal into bowls. As she sprinkles cinnamon on top, she says, "Doesn't Asger work nights at the casino?"

"His schedule varies. He's on the day shift for the next couple of weeks. Same with the other guys in the band. One of them, Raphael, is a croupier at the casino." I tap my lip with my finger. "Actually, I'm not sure what J.B. does for a living, but Asger did say he's free at night."

Pedro helps Grace carry the oatmeal and bacon over to the kitchen island. "Sounds like it's doable."

Sebastien nods. "But I worry about you, Jasmine. Rehearsing day and night. It's a lot. Are you sure you can manage?"

"It's only for a few weeks," I say. "It'll be like the old days when I was juggling a lot of balls–the symphony, teaching private lessons, playing with other groups, all that. I think I can manage. Asger was always there for me in high school. Now I have a chance to be there for him."

"Did he like the dress?" Sebastien asks as he pours heavy cream on his oatmeal.

I furrow my brow. "The dress?"

"You know, the sexy number you were wearing last night," Sebastien says with a sly smile.

I scowl at him. "He didn't say anything about the dress."

"Really?" Sebastien takes a bite of his oatmeal and gives Grace a thumbs up. Then he looks back at me. "I bet he noticed the dress, though."

"It was just a dress."

"A sexy dress."

"Oh, my gosh, can you please drop it," I say.

Sebastien grins at me. "Probably not."

Thankfully, Pedro interrupts Sebastien's annoying comments about my dress. "Does being in the country band mean you're going to get one of those cool sequined cowboy hats?"

When I groan, Grace laughs. "You didn't think this through, did you? Not only do you get to play the fiddle, you also get to wear cowgirl clothes."

"I love costumes," Pedro says. "We should do that. How about Star Wars outfits? Sebastien could dress up as Chewbacca, Grace would make a great Princess Leia, Jasmine would look cool as Ahsoka Tano, and I can be Obi Wan Kenobi."

Grace squashes this idea immediately. "We're a string quartet, not trick or treaters at Halloween."

"I sweat easily," Sebastien says. "I think a Chewbacca costume is going to be too hot."

Pedro considers this, then says, "How about Han Solo?"

"I can get on board with that." Sebastien nods. "I like his blasters."

Grace looks like her head is going to explode. "We are not wearing costumes," she says emphatically.

"We're just kidding around," Sebastien says.

Pedro shakes his head. "I wasn't."

Thinking back to the red dress I wore to the casino for my blind date, I say, "While I'm with Grace on the no costume thing, maybe we could wear something other than black."

Grace initially concedes this point, but when Pedro asks if this means he can wear a velvet rainbow-striped tuxedo, she retracts her support. "Let's stick to black for now, okay?"

Pedro looks crestfallen, but he agrees. As we finish our oatmeal and bacon, Sebastien reminds us that we're starting rehearsal in an hour.

"Are you rehearsing with your other band today?" Sebastien asks me.

"Yes, at six." I start to clear the dishes, then turn to look back at the others. "That's assuming you're all okay with me helping Whiskey and Bragi out."

"Um, before you say yes," Grace says. "Jasmine left out one vital piece of information about her plan that you should be aware of."

Both Sebastien and Pedro fix their gaze on me. I shrug. "It's not really a big deal. Just some silly bureaucratic nonsense with the competition rules."

"Jasmine has to pretend to be Terese," Grace says. "If they find out it's Jasmine playing fiddle instead of Terese, Whiskey and Bragi will be disqualified."

To no one's surprise, Pedro is thrilled with this idea. "It's like one of those undercover shows I like to stream. Are you going to wear a disguise?"

Sebastien looks amused. "You must really like this guy."

Grace nods. "That's what I told her, but she's denying it."

"He's just a friend." I put my hands on my hips. "I'd do the same for any of you."

Sebastien carries over the coffee cups to the counter, then pats me on the shoulder. "Sure. We believe you. Not."

* * *

We practice Shostakovich's String Quartet No. 8 in C Minor for a couple of hours after breakfast. It's a haunting piece of music, especially the first movement. It amazes me that the Russian composer wrote it in three days. I'm in awe of anyone who can compose music, whether that be a classical score or a country tune.

As we break for lunch, I think about the bluegrass inspired melody I heard Asger singing the other day. I wonder if it was a cover or something he composed himself. His vocals had been sensational, and the rest of the band was top-notch.

Anxiety bubbles up inside me. What was I thinking, volunteering to play with them? There's no way I can perform at their level. A classical musician masquerading as a country fiddler? No one is going to buy it.

I grab a quick bite to eat, then go up to my room and try to meditate my fears away. But instead of releasing my negative thoughts, I only work myself up some more. I'm not sure what's bothering me more–

making a fool of myself up on stage or disappointing Asger.

"What do you think, Joshua?" I ask my violin. "Should I back out? Should I tell Asger to find another person to fill in for Terese?"

But as usual, Joshua keeps his thoughts to himself. I wonder what the real Joshua Bell would do in this situation?

"Jasmine? Are you coming?" Grace calls out. "We're getting ready to start."

"On my way." I tuck Joshua back in his case, then carry him downstairs. When I walk into the music room, I apologize for being late.

"No problem, we're waiting for our guest to arrive," Sebastien says.

"What guest?" I'm a bit taken aback as we usually have closed rehearsals.

"Ah, here he is," Sebastien says. "Allow me to introduce the birthday boy, Prince Oboroten."

As the prince shakes hands with Pedro, I take a moment to observe the man we'll be playing for on Saturday. He's in his forties, tall and lean, with dark wavy hair cascading to his shoulders and piercing violet eyes. The casual clothes he's wearing look like something you can buy off the rack–dark jeans, a fitted gray t-shirt, and sneakers. But the Patek Philippe watch on his wrist is something only the most wealthy can afford.

After a brief conversation with Pedro about

Mexico's chances in the next World Cup, the prince turns to Grace. He takes her hand in his and kisses the back of it, then charms her with his knowledge of her hometown on Prince Edward's Island.

Finally, it's my turn. When he smiles at me, I melt a little. This guy might just be my Prince Charming–rich, good-looking, and a lover of classical music.

Is it my imagination or do his lips linger on the back of my hand?

"Sebastien has told me so much about you," he says. "You share the same name as my favorite flower."

"I think my parents named me after the Disney character," I say.

He smiles. "Ah, yes, Princess Jasmine from the movie *Aladdin*."

I like how that sounds–Princess Jasmine. A royal title in front of my name? Yes, please.

"Do you prefer the original movie or the remake?" the prince asks me.

"I've never seen the remake," I confess.

Pedro claps his hands. "Let's have a movie night. We can watch both versions. Ooh. How about if we wear–"

Grace holds up her hand. "No costumes."

The prince looks bemused as Pedro's shoulders slump. "I think it's an excellent idea," he says. When Grace's eyes widen, he adds, "Not the costumes, but a movie night. I would be delighted to host all of you."

"Obie does have a nice in-home theater," Sebastien says.

I tilt my head to one side. "Obie?"

"Oboroten is a mouthful," the prince says. "So my friends call me Obie instead. And since you are all now my friends, please call me Obie."

Sebastien motions over to the other side of the room where chairs and music stands are set up. "We need to get started. Obie wants to hear what we're planning on playing at his party."

While the prince and Sebastien discuss whether we should start with the Shostakovich piece or the Rachmaninoff one, I put rosin on my bow, then start to tune my violin. As I'm tightening one of the strings the prince walks toward me.

He stares at my violin. His voice is low and husky as he asks, "Is that an Avestruz?"

"It is," I say. "I'm surprised you recognize it."

"This is the first one I've seen in person. It's exquisite." The prince extends his hand. "May I?"

I hesitate. I'm reluctant to let anyone hold my violin. But when I see Sebastien give me an encouraging nod, I hand it to the prince. "Please, be careful."

"Of course, I know how valuable this instrument is." He looks reverent as he examines my pride and joy. As he gently traces the violin's figure eight shape with his fingers, he says, "The workmanship is unparalleled. How did it come to be in your possession?"

"It's a long story," I say.

"I would love to hear it." He looks at me, the violet in his eyes even more intense than before. "Perhaps over a drink tonight?"

"I'd love to . . ." Remembering I have rehearsal with Whiskey and Bragi tonight, I frown. "I'm pretty tied up for the next few nights, but maybe another time?"

"Tomorrow afternoon?" the prince suggests.

I look at Sebastien and he shrugs. "We finish rehearsal at three tomorrow."

"Perfect. We have a lot to talk about." As I go to take my violin back, the prince adds, "Including what this violin is worth to you."

"It's priceless," I say, feeling relieved Joshua is back in my arms where he belongs.

I feel a chill go down my spine as the prince leans down and whispers in my ear, "My dear, everyone and everything has a price, including this Avestruz."

CHAPTER 6
THE ONE ABOUT THE WISHBONE

I take a taxi to Asger's that night. There's no way I'm going to carry Joshua through the streets of Monaco. The way Prince Oboroten looked at my violin earlier in the day, with desire flashing in his eyes, made me feel uneasy. It's unleashed a protective instinct inside me that I didn't realize was there.

The prince had remarked on how valuable my violin was, and he's right it is. Not in a monetary sense, really. Unlike Stradivarius or Guarneri violins, Avestruz violins are relatively unknown. Avestruz had originally been a cobbler in the Australian outback in the 1970s. But as fewer and fewer people brought their shoes to him to be repaired, he turned to refurbishing musical instruments. Eventually, that led to him making his first violin, followed by five more before he died.

Avestruz refused to let anyone play his violins, instead displaying them in his garage over his woodworking tools. After his passing, his widow took them to a second-hand shop. To her, they were just more clutter that she had to deal with. Fortunately, a violinist on vacation spotted them. He was intrigued by the kangaroo and koala engravings, snapping up all six violins on a lark. Once he played them, he realized that their workmanship and musical quality were exceptional.

Avestruz violins are still relatively unknown, but a cult following is starting to develop. I consider myself lucky to be the owner of one of them. No one is going to take mine away from me, not even if they have royal blood.

When I get out of the taxi at Asger's place, I clutch my violin case close to my body until I'm inside. J.B. makes a whooping noise when he spots me. He slaps Raphael on the back. "See, I told you she'd show."

Raphael kisses me on both cheeks as he apologizes for thinking I'd chicken out. When I tell him I almost did, he whistles. "Asger would have been devastated."

"Where is he?" I ask, looking around the converted garage.

"He's running late, but he'll be here soon." J.B. rubs his hands together. "But as long as he's not here, you can give us the scoop on what he was like when he was a teenager. The more embarrassing the stories are, the better."

"I wouldn't do that to Asger," I say. "Unless, of course, you have something to trade. Got any good dirt?"

J.B. gives me a high five. "I like the way you think."

Raphael hands me a soda while I think about what story to share. I take a sip of the cola, then say, "I've got a turkey day one."

"Turkey day?" Raphael asks. "What is this?"

"She means Thanksgiving," J.B. explains.

"That's right," I say. "There really isn't a French equivalent, is there?"

"No. But I've seen it on *Friends*," he says. "Chandler kissed Joey's girlfriend, so Chandler locked him in a box for Thanksgiving. It was an interesting insight into American culture."

"Yeah, man, you should never kiss another guy's girl," J.B. says before turning to me. "Okay, let's hear the juicy gossip."

As I perch on the arm of the tattered couch, the guys look at me expectantly. "Well, Asger's host parents were going to visit their daughter and son-in-law for Thanksgiving. She had just had a baby and couldn't travel. Asger was invited to join them, but he didn't want to intrude, so my parents invited him to stay with us for the holiday weekend."

I look at Raphael. "Do you know what a wishbone is?"

"Is it like a funny bone?" he asks.

"That's actually a nerve in your elbow. The wishbone is in the turkey's neck. It's V-shaped." J.B. demonstrates with his hands. "Each person holds one side of the bone using their pinky finger. Then they both pull their hands apart, snapping the bone in two. If you get the bigger piece of bone, then your wish comes true."

Raphael wrinkles his nose. "Americans are weird."

"I won't argue with you there," J.B. says.

"Asger thought the same thing," I say. "Especially when my mom put the wishbone in the dishwasher so that it would dry out. It doesn't work unless the bone is dry, and we didn't want to wait a few days for it to dry naturally. Anyway, Asger and I did the wishbone later that night, after we had our pumpkin pie."

J.B. folds his arms across his chest. "So far, this is a pretty normal story. I'm not hearing anything embarrassing yet."

"Never fear, it gets good. The next morning, Asger got up before everyone else. My mom had saved the turkey carcass to make soup with and . . ." I pause for dramatic effect, but before I can finish my story, J.B. bursts out laughing.

"Don't tell me he put the carcass in the dishwasher," he says.

"Yep. My dad had made a joke about pulling apart the carcass for even better luck on Black Friday, and Asger thought he was serious. So after he unloaded the dishwasher, he stuck the rest of the bird inside."

J.B.'s laughter is contagious. It takes ages before I stop howling. As I wipe tears from my eyes, I say, "Thankfully, my mom came down before he started the dishwasher."

"I can't believe you told them the turkey story." Asger is standing in the doorway. He's traded in his Dolly Parton t-shirt for a Kenny Rogers one. I'm beginning to wonder about his wardrobe. Does it consist entirely of shirts with the faces of country music stars plastered on them? "Do you want me to tell them about the time you and the high school mascot-"

I rush over to Asger and put my hand over his mouth. "Please, I'm begging you."

He squirms away from me, darting back and forth around the garage. I chase after him, tugging on the hem of his t-shirt until he stops. He spins around and puts his hands on my waist. "What's it worth to you?"

I smile at him sweetly. "How about if I play the fiddle in your band?"

He laughs. "Deal."

As he releases me, I'm conscious of the fact that J.B. and Raphael are in the room. If they hadn't been, I might have offered something else in exchange for his silence, like a kiss.

Grateful their presence saved me from making a fool out of myself, I go and get Joshua out of his case. I rub the koala and kangaroo engravings for good luck, then we start rehearsal. It's such a different experience than playing with the quartet. The guys banter constantly with each other. The atmosphere is light-hearted, like a bunch of folks jamming for the fun of it.

Not that rehearsals with the quartet aren't fun. We all enjoy each other's company, and Pedro always provides moments of comic relief. But Sebastien runs a tight ship, taking his role as our leader seriously.

The other big difference is the fact that they have a singer. The heart and soul of Whiskey and Bragi's music is the power of Asger's voice. That sexy twangy growl when he hits the low notes, and the brightness of his high notes takes my breath away. I need to remind myself to stop looking at him and concentrate on the sheet music instead.

When Asger sings a line about friends becoming lovers, my stomach flutters and I mess up my part. The guys are gracious about it, suggesting we take a break.

"Who wants a beer?" Asger asks. We all raise our hands. When he returns with frosty bottles of Stella Artois and a bag of potato chips, I smile to myself. Just a couple of nights ago, I was thrilled to be at a fancy bar sipping on champagne and sampling caviar. Now here I am, in a garage, drinking beer and eating chips.

As if reading my mind, Asger smiles at me. When it comes to high school reunions, this one is turning out to be a good one.

* * *

The next day, after our quartet rehearsal wraps up for the afternoon, I take my violin case upstairs. As I'm tucking it underneath my bed for safekeeping, I tell Joshua that I'll be back in a couple of hours.

Yes, I know talking to a violin is odd. But to a musician, their instrument is an extension of themselves, so I'm really talking to myself. Okay, that's odd as well. But what hasn't been odd about the past few days?

Mentally shaking myself, I go to get ready for my appointment with the prince. Because that's what this is–an appointment, not a date. Although I initially thought Obie could be my Prince Charming, the way he looked at Joshua yesterday creeped me out.

I trade out my jeans and t-shirt for a flowy skirt and embroidered peasant blouse. It's a cute outfit, but nothing that would be mistaken for something you wear to impress a date. Because the last thing I need is for Sebastien to start winding me up about my fashion choices.

I sneak out of the villa without saying goodbye to the others, then walk the short distance to where the prince lives. Although it's much larger, the outside of the building looks similar to Sebastien's place–marble columns, lots of balconies, French windows, and a grand entrance. But the difference when I walk inside is immediate. Every imaginable surface is gilded or mirrored, making me wish I had worn sunglasses.

The maid ushers me into a sitting room which is decorated in leopard print. So much leopard print. Now I feel like I should be wearing some sort of safari suit. The only relief from the black and caramel pattern is a large portrait of the prince hanging over the onyx fireplace. But even in that, he's standing on a leopard skin rug and wearing a leopard print cape.

"Do you like it?" I hear the prince say behind me.

I hesitate before turning. Is he asking about the interior decorating choices he's made or about the painting of him? What can I say that's nice about either of them?

"I don't think I've ever seen anything quite like it," I say as I spin around.

The prince beams. "Let me give you a tour of the rest of the villa. I think you'll be impressed."

As he leads me back out into the gilded and mirrored hall, I ask him why he doesn't live in a castle. "You're royal," I say. "I thought castles came with the job."

"Don't worry. I have a castle. Two, in fact." The prince pauses next to a statue of the Greek god Dionysus and scratches his head. "Actually, make that three."

"I can't imagine losing track of how many castles I own," I say dryly.

"It happens to the best of us," he says without the slightest bit of irony. "How about some champagne before we start the tour?"

"I wouldn't say no."

The prince snaps his fingers. Seconds later, the maid appears with two champagne flutes. It's like speed dial for the rich. With my glass in hand, I follow the prince down the long hall and out onto a terrace.

He points at a large sunken pool surrounded by a perfectly manicured lawn. Swimming around the pool is a pair of swans. "I won them in a poker match."

"You gamble for birds?"

"Sure. Swans and flamingos are good. Pigeons, not so much." He takes a sip of his champagne. "How about you? Do you like poker?"

"Never played."

"Really? I'll teach you. There's a private game every Thursday. Very exclusive crowd, but I can get you in." He looks me up and down as though he's appraising a race horse. "I like to have a pretty girl on my arm for good luck."

I take a few steps back. "I don't know. I think I'll stick to the occasional scratch card."

"Don't be silly. Scratch cards are for peasants." He snaps his fingers, and a maid appears with a bottle of champagne. After she tops up our glasses, the prince tells me to follow him. "I will show you my collection now."

"Your collection of what?"

"Anything that catches my interest," he says over his shoulder. "Let's start with the cars."

The prince's garage is a large, climate-controlled structure. There are over twenty vehicles parked inside the spotless facility. Some look like antiques, others are so futuristic that I wonder if they're capable of interstellar travel.

He pauses in front of a neon-pink race car. "This one is my new favorite. I plan on racing it in the Grand Prix next year."

"You're a Formula 1 driver?"

"It's my new hobby."

Thinking back to the displays at the café Asger took me to the other night, I say, "I thought qualifying to be a Formula 1 driver took years. Aren't there a lot of requirements you have to meet?"

The prince chuckles. "People with money don't have to follow the rules. They make the rules."

My stomach clenches as I think about how I'm breaking the country music competition rules by pretending to be Terese. Something like that wouldn't even phase the prince.

"I don't know. It seems pretty dangerous," I say. "The last hobby I took up was knitting."

The prince frowns as I run my hand along the side of the race car. He snaps his fingers and a man wearing blue coveralls rushes up and wipes away my fingerprints with a cloth. I apologize as I back away.

"Let me show you something that might be more to your liking," he says.

We walk over to the far side of the garage and I

squeal with delight when the prince points at a tiny light blue convertible. "It's adorable."

"Are you familiar with the Citröen deux chevaux? They are French cars. This particular one was made in 1950." As the prince pats the canvas top, he tells me that its top speed is around forty miles per hour. "Perfect for someone who is scared of living dangerously."

"Guilty." I finish the rest of my champagne while the prince tells me more trivia about the production of Citröen cars. To be honest, I'm barely paying attention to what he says. Cars hold zero interest for me. It's only when the prince snaps his fingers that I tune back in.

As the man in coveralls takes our glasses, the prince tells me that he is going to give the Citröen to me.

"What?" I splutter.

"I don't like the color," he says matter-of-factly. "Would you like to drive it back to Sebastien's, or should I have it delivered? The keys are already in the ignition."

I hold my hands up. "Neither. I can't accept this."

The prince furrows his brow. "Why not?"

"Because it's, um, a car."

"Hmm." He shrugs. "Okay, I'll give it to someone else."

Then the prince whisks me back inside the villa. A glass elevator takes us to the top floor of his villa. He presses his right eye against a scanner on the wall, then a heavy metal door swings open. "Welcome to my gallery."

I know that the prince is a friend of Sebastien's and that he's hired our quartet to play at his party tomorrow night, but this is all getting to be a bit much. "You know, I actually need to get going. I have rehearsal in an hour."

"Rehearsal? I thought you already rehearsed with the quartet."

"This is another group I'm in."

"You musicians are such busy people." He rubs his hands together. "Okay, we will make it a quick tour."

As we walk into the gallery, I notice a familiar looking painting. "Isn't that a Monet?"

"Yes, do you like it?"

Worried that the prince will try to gift it to me, I tell him that I'm not a fan of lily pads. "Something about the way they float on the water freaks me out. It's a very good reproduction, though."

The prince presses his lips together. "It's not a reproduction."

"I could swear I saw this at the Louvre." I take a closer look at the brush strokes. "Maybe it was a different one, though."

"Perhaps it's best if you don't tell anyone that you saw this painting here." The prince grabs my hand and quickly leads me into the next room. "Here is where I keep my collection of musical instruments. I have just the spot for the Avestruz. Right here next to the harpsichord."

I yank my hand away. "Like I told you yesterday, my violin is not for sale."

"No, what you said was that your violin was priceless. But that's not true, is it, my dear? We just need to figure out what the right price is." He narrows his eyes. "I always get what I want. Only you can decide how pleasant of an experience it will be."

CHAPTER 7
THE TATER TOT PLAYLIST

"I'm not looking forward to playing at the prince's birthday party tonight," I say to Sebastien the next afternoon. We're sitting on a bench in the Princess Grace Rose Garden near a picturesque bronze fountain. The scent of the roses is heavenly, but I don't let it distract me from telling Sebastien about my concerns. "He's fixated on my violin. I told him repeatedly that it's not for sale, but he won't take no for an answer."

Sebastien frowns. "He does have rather an obsessive personality."

"I know he's a good friend of yours, but . . ."

"Our families are friends. We run in the same social circles. I've known him forever," Sebastien explains. "But would I consider him a good friend? No."

"I'm probably overreacting," I say. "I'm sure the party will be fine."

"If you're concerned, then I'm concerned." Sebastien squeezes my hand. "Unlike Obie, you are a good friend of mine."

"Thanks. Just hearing you say that makes me feel better." I smile. "He reminds me of a weird James Bond villain."

Sebastien chuckles. "He would take that as a compliment."

"And his villa. What's up with all the leopard print?"

"That's new. Last time I was there, it was all about stainless steel and these strange plaid throw pillows. He redecorates a lot," Sebastien says. "That's the thing with Obie. He gets bored easily. This obsession with your violin won't last long. Then he'll be on to the next thing."

"I guess he does have one redeeming quality–he loves classical music."

"He pretends to love classical music. Big difference."

"Another obsession?"

"Yeah. A few months ago it was K-pop."

I wipe a bead of sweat off my brow, then tuck one of my legs under me as I try to get more comfortable on the hard bench. "It's a shame you don't know any normal rich guys."

"I do, but they're all taken." Sebastien smiles at me, then his expression turns more serious. "I get that what happened to you with your ex really scarred you, but I don't think the answer is trying to find a husband with money."

I tip my head back and exhale slowly. "I can't go through that again. He took every penny I had."

"But you're back on your feet now," Sebastien says.

"Barely. I still have a massive credit card debt."

"You know I'm happy to–"

Twisting around on the bench, I cut Sebastien off. "It's bad enough you gave me the money to pay back Asger. I won't have you taking care of my credit card, too."

Sebastien gives me a look. "Playing devil's advocate here. Is it okay if you marry someone and he pays off your debt?"

I put my face into my hands. "Ugh. Why do you have to say things I don't want to hear?"

Thankfully, he doesn't press me. I'm not sure what I would say if he did. Admitting that I'm a hot mess, who thinks a rich guy can save me, isn't something I want to say out loud. Starting with my on and off again relationship with Corey in high school, my dating life has continued to be a disaster.

There was the guy in college who cheated on me during my sophomore year. Later, there was the oboe player who ghosted me after introducing me to his parents. Then a couple of men I met on dating apps whose profiles didn't even come close to matching reality. All of it culminating in a whirlwind marriage that plunged me into financial chaos and heartbreak.

"How's Asger?" Sebastien asks, interrupting my thoughts.

"Fine. He seemed happy with how rehearsal went yesterday."

"That's not exactly what I was asking."

I roll my eyes. "You're not going to start talking about my dress again, are you?"

"Admit it, you like him." He waves a finger at me. "And I don't mean as friends. You're interested in him romantically."

"If I confess to being attracted to him, will that get you to drop the subject?"

Sebastien gives me a cocky grin. "Nah. We're just getting started. Let's begin with what you like about him."

Sometimes, it's easier to give in when it comes to Sebastien. The man can be relentless when he wants to know something. I let out a deep sigh, then start listing Asger's qualities. "He's fun to be with and easy to talk to. I feel comfortable around him. He's one of those guys that will do anything for you. Whenever you're in trouble, he's there to help."

A little boy races past us, screaming at the top of his lungs, distracting me for a moment. His mother chases after him, scooping him up into her arms, then tickling his belly. It's a cute moment.

Sebastien smiles at the two of them, then turns back to me. "Do you want kids?"

I nod. "One of these days."

"When you think of Asger, can you picture him as a dad?"

I burst out laughing. "You missed your calling. Instead of being a musician, you should have been a therapist. All these deep questions of yours. You gotta stop reading all those self-help books."

He looks sheepish. "Fair point."

"Makes me wonder if these are questions you're asking yourself," I point out.

"Probably," he says softly. Then he gets up and pulls me to my feet. "We should head back."

As we walk through the garden, our conversation turns to music. It's a safe topic, one we're both comfortable with.

"Tell me about the type of songs Whiskey and Bragi plays," Sebastien asks me. "I don't know much about country music."

"Me neither," I say. "From what I can figure out, Asger's band has an eclectic kind of style. It's a mix of bluegrass, western swing, country pop, and a bunch of other stuff I couldn't tell you about."

"Do they mostly do covers?"

"It's a mix of covers and original songs that Asger wrote," I say. "They have a big repertoire. Fortunately, for the competition, I only have to learn four songs. One original and three covers. My favorite cover is an Alabama one. The lyrics are about how you need a fiddle in the band if you're going to play in Texas. It's a toe-tapper."

Sebastien grins. "Should I be worried that you're going to ditch our quartet and become a country musician?"

"No, my heart will always be with classical music," I say. "But it's been fun experimenting with country songs."

"It'll probably make you a better violinist," Sebastien muses. "We should think about exploring other musical styles in our rehearsals. Not necessarily to perform, but to keep things fresh."

"Good luck getting Grace on board with that. You know what a snob she is when it comes to music."

"Leave her to me," Sebastien says. "Now, tell me about the songs Asger composed."

"They're both ballads. And when Asger sings them, it makes me . . ." My voice trails off as I struggle to put into words how Asger's lyrics affect me.

"Makes you what?" Sebastien prompts

"It makes me feel all the things." I clear my throat. "Sorry, I can't explain it any other way than that."

Sebastien gives me a gentle smile. "Feeling all the things works."

We stop in front of a bronze statue of Princess Grace. "It was created by the sculptor Kees Verkade in 1983," Sebastien tells me.

"She was so elegant," I say. "And she found her Prince Charming."

"Have you ever see any of her movies?"

"My friend Olivia has an aunt who adores old movies," I say. "Whenever her aunt Celeste came to visit, she'd have a movie night with me and Olivia. I remember the time we watched *To Catch a Thief*. It starred Cary Grant along with Grace Kelly."

"Is that the one about the retired cat burglar?" Sebastien asks. "There's that scene where Cary Grant's character is sneaking around the rooftop. Even though I knew it was a film, I was scared he was going to fall."

"That's the one." I close my eyes as I try to recall the details of the scene. I remember Celeste being wistful as we watched the movie. Olivia told me later that her aunt had been involved in an ill-fated relationship with a jewel thief. But she had later gone on to marry the love of her life. Maybe there was hope for me after all.

"We should have a movie night when I get back and rewatch *To Catch a Thief*," Sebastien suggests.

"That would be good, as long as we don't have to invite Obie." I shake my head. "You don't think he was serious about having an *Aladdin* movie night at his villa, do you?"

"He's probably forgotten all about it," Sebastien says.

"I hope so," I say. "And I hope he's forgotten all about my violin, too."

* * *

Later that night, we arrive at the venue the prince has rented for his birthday party. Sebastien, Pedro, and Grace decide to hang out in the greenroom while we wait to perform. I entrust Joshua to their safekeeping while I go exploring.

The banquet room where the event will take place is absolutely stunning with its Belle Époque architecture and decor. I walk around the space admiring the pink marble columns, the gilded wood paneling, and the sparkling crystal chandeliers. Then I come to a screeching halt as I see someone carrying a pile of leopard print tablecloths into the room.

If there was a way to ruin the elegant atmosphere, it would be with leopard print. Let's just hope that the birthday boy isn't planning on matching his clothes to the tablecloths.

Oh, too late. I spy the prince in the corner of the room, conferring with one of the catering staff. He's dressed head to toe in a leopard print three piece suit. Even his shoes have that familiar caramel and black pattern on them. Well, I guess if you have a look you love, why not go all in?

I do a double take when I realize the man the prince is speaking with is J.B. Because my quartet is playing at the birthday party, Whiskey and Bragi has the night off from rehearsal. J.B. had mentioned that he had picked up a shift at an event. What are the odds it would be this one?

I have mixed feelings about J.B. being here. It's always nice to have a friendly face in the audience, but I also feel a little weird having him hear me play classical music. It's like I have two personalities—a free and loose country music chick and a more restrained violinist whose black dress blends into the background.

Thankfully, the prince doesn't notice me. The fact that I'm lurking behind one of the marble columns probably helps. When he leaves the room, I walk over to say hi to J.B.

"Are you the entertainment tonight?" he asks. "I knew he was having music, but I thought it was supposed to be a K-pop band."

"Apparently, that's so last year for the prince." As J.B. unfolds one of the leopard print tablecloths, I add, "I'm surprised he's not having some sort of circus act with actual leopards instead of a string quartet."

J.B. chuckles "Oh, he tried. But there was some problem with the import license."

"The prince doesn't strike me as a rule follower. But I suppose sneaking a leopard into the country might be harder than, say, stealing a painting from the Louvre." When J.B. gives me a funny look, I wave a hand in the air. "Never mind. It's a long story."

"Oh, no." J.B. frowns. "I can't believe she's here."

"Who?" I turn to see who J.B. is staring at. "Wait a minute, is that Terese?"

"She does catering gigs, too," J.B. explains. "But I haven't seen her since she quit the band. This is going to be awkward."

"Maybe you can talk her into coming back?" My voice does a weird inflection thing at the end, making what I've said a sort of half-question, half-statement. It reflects what I'm feeling. The easiest thing for me would be for Terese to rejoin Whiskey and Bragi. She's a country fiddler, through and through. I'm just a classical violinist masquerading as one.

On the other hand, I've been loving rehearsing with the band over the past couple of days. I kind of want to see it through. Naturally, once the competition is over, I'll go back to focusing on my classical stuff. But in the meantime, I'm having fun . . . although the thought of having to wear a sequined cowboy hat makes me cringe.

Terese sashays over to us, her eyes darting back and forth between J.B. and me. I take the opportunity to study her face and hair so that I can replicate it for the Riviera Musical Rodeo. She certainly doesn't skimp on her eyeliner or mascara, and the deep purple eyeshadow she's wearing makes her eyes pop. Way too much blush for my liking, but I do think her plum colored lip gloss is nice.

I wonder how much it's going to cost me in

cosmetics to mirror her look. My credit card is already screaming at me. Fortunately, when it comes to Terese's hairstyle, I shouldn't need any special products. She wears it long with soft curls. While I usually wear my hair in an updo when I'm performing or pulled back during the day, curling it and wearing it down is often my go-to look at night.

J.B. asks Terese how she's doing, but rather than answer him, she turns and glares at me. "I hear you're taking my place."

"Um, yeah," I say, more defensively than I would have liked.

"You're never going to pull it off," she sneers.

J.B. jumps in to support me. "Jasmine is a quick study. She's going to do a great job."

I take a deep breath, then hold out an olive branch. "I'll never be as good as you are, that's true. Whiskey and Bragi have a much better chance of winning with you. I know they'd love to have you back."

"Speak for yourself," J.B. mutters under his breath.

Terese narrows her eyes. "No. I'm done with all that now."

"This is about your boyfriend, isn't it?" I ask. "I get that he wants you to spend more time with him, but it would just be for a couple of weeks. Just until after the competition."

"I'm the one who made the decision." Terese pats her chest. "Me. Not him."

"Sorry," I say. "I wasn't trying to imply that he was

controlling you. It's obvious that you're not a pushover."

"Damn right." Terese looks me up and down. "Why are you here, anyway? Are you a guest?"

I shake my head. "I'm part of the string quartet that's playing tonight."

"I thought they were having a K-pop band," Terese says. "They're serving bulgogi and kimchi for dinner. Not really the type of cuisine that goes with a lame classical music quartet."

I arch an eyebrow. "Classical music goes with everything."

"Even tater tots?" Terese asks, her voice dripping with sarcasm.

"Especially tater tots." I square up my shoulders. "I can send you a playlist if you want."

J.B. holds up his hands. "Okay, ladies. Maybe we can talk about this another time. I'm sure Jasmine needs to get ready, and we need to get the tables laid before the guests start arriving."

"I hope you won't get nervous knowing I'm watching you play," Terese says, her eyes cold and hard.

I lift my chin. "I'm never nervous when I'm with Joshua."

"That your boyfriend?" she asks.

"No, Joshua is my violin."

Terese snorts derisively. "That's a stupid name."

"What do you call your fiddle?"

"None of your business."

J.B. eyes us warily, then says, "Jasmine's violin is really cool. It has an kangaroo and a koala engraved on it."

Terese gasps. "You own an Avestruz?"

"I do," I say slowly.

"Those are worth a lot of money to the right buyer," she says. "If you need to make some quick cash, let me know and I can hook you up."

"Joshua is not for sale."

Terese shrugs. "Whatever."

"Okay, seriously, we need to get to work," J.B. says to her. "Why don't I start doing the tables at this side of the room and you work on those ones over there?"

While he gets to work making the table look like it's straight out of a show on The Animal Channel, I walk toward the exit. Terese intercepts me, yanking my arm sharply. "You want to make sure you stay on my good side," she says in an undertone. "I know about the competition rules. If they find out you're pretending to be me, the band gets disqualified. You wouldn't want that to happen, would you?"

CHAPTER 8
VIKING COWBOYS

Two weeks later, I'm backstage in the greenroom at the Rainier III Auditorium. This venue is where the Orchestre Philharmonique de Monaco normally plays, but instead of classical music, tonight it's hosting the Riviera Musical Rodeo. The place is packed with country music fans from around the world. If this event is successful, Monte Carlo might very well become the Nashville of Europe.

While I pace back and forth, the rest of the band looks relaxed. J.B. and Raphael are over by the hospitality table. Asger is standing near me, adjusting the strap on his guitar.

"How long until things kick off?" I set my violin case down on the floor and rub my fingers.

"It won't be too long." Asger shifts his guitar, then

looks up at me. "You okay, Jasmine?"

"Not really. I wish I hadn't eaten that pizza."

Asger closes the distance between us, then gently tilts my face up so that I'm looking at him. "Hey, you're going to be fine. You've nailed everything in rehearsal, and you'll do the same on stage."

"I don't want to mess this up for you," I say softly. "This could be your big break."

He chuckles. "You mean *our* big break."

"This is a one-time thing," I say. "You know that."

"What can I do to change your mind?" Asger runs his fingers lightly along my cheek. "We make a great team."

"You'll find someone else to play fiddle." I take a step back before the sensation of Asger touching my face overwhelms me. Motioning at the other bands in the vicinity, I say, "Maybe you can poach one of their fiddle players."

"Poaching isn't my style."

I arch an eyebrow. "Really? Weren't you the guy who just tried to poach me from Sebastien's quartet?"

He grins at me. "Fair point. I'd like to meet Sebastien and the others one of these days."

"Um, yeah, we should do that," I say warily. The thought of what Sebastien might do if the two groups met face-to-face gives me pause. It'd be like a bad episode of *Monte Carlo Matchmaker* with Sebastien determined to set Asger and me up. Would Grace be able to mask her disdain for country music? Pedro would be the easy one, probably wearing a cowboy costume in Whiskey and Bragi's honor.

"Are they here tonight?" Asger asks.

"They were threatening to come, but tickets were hard to get," I say. "Sebastien was going to see if he could pull a few strings. But no one seems to know who the organizer of the event is, other than the fact that it's some billionaire."

"All will be revealed soon." Asger looks at his phone. "Fifteen minutes until the curtain goes up."

"There's nine bands before us, right?" I ask. "I wonder how long it will take until we go on?"

"Well, each band is doing two songs tonight during this round. So, factoring in introductions and getting set up on stage, we're probably looking at six, seven minutes per band . . ."

I smile as Asger pauses to do some mental calculations. "It's okay. I don't really need to know. I'm just glad we're on before intermission. Of course, then there's all the waiting around until they announce which three bands are going through to the finals next weekend."

"You mean which two bands are going to join us in the finals," Asger says with an air of confidence.

"See, now you're making me nervous again. If Whiskey and Bragi don't get through, it will be because of me."

"If we win, it will be *because* of you. Not only are you an incredibly talented musician, you look amazing in that hat."

I roll my eyes. Imagine if you took a bunch of Vikings, put them on the set of *Barbie*, then sprinkled them with sequins. That would sum up the ridiculous costumes we're wearing. Hot pink fringed shirts with Scandinavian runes embroidered on the yokes. Plastic battle axes in our low slung holsters. Large belt buckles with Thor's hammer. And the pièce de résistance–the large sequined cowboy hats with Viking horns attached to the sides. The only normal thing about what we're wearing are our cowboy boots.

Asger thinks our outfits will make us stand out. He's not wrong there. Who knows? Maybe Viking country music is the wave of the future.

J.B. walks toward us, a worried expression on his face. "I think we have a problem," he says to me. "See that man that just walked in? Isn't that Leopard Guy?"

"Who's Leopard Guy?" Asger asks.

I pull the brim of my hat low over my face, then slowly turn to see if my nightmare is about to come true . . . and it has.

Prince Oboroten is standing in the greenroom doorway talking with one of the stage runners. He's dressed head-to-toe in leopard print, much like the night of his birthday party. Except this time, instead of understated caramel and black spots, the fabric that his suit is made out of is iridescent and the pattern is fluorescent lime-green and purple.

Okay, maybe we aren't the most ridiculously dressed people here.

"Why is he here?" I whisper to J.B.

J.B. shakes his head. "I don't know, but if he sees you–"

"What is going on?" Asger asks.

"Shush, lower your voice." I position myself so that J.B. blocks the prince's view of me. "That's who we played for at the birthday party. He knows who I am. If he sees me, he could blow my cover."

"Just play it cool," J.B. says to me. "He's probably here visiting someone he knows in another band. He'll be gone soon."

"But he's obviously here to see the competition. If he tells anyone I'm not Terese, we could be eliminated," I splutter.

"I think you'll be okay. It's all about context, right? Leopard Guy associates you with classical music." J.B. waves a hand at me. "Between your heavy makeup and this outfit, he won't place you. Just keep your hat down low like you have it now and stay in the background."

I see Raphael motioning to us from the hospitality table to see if we want anything to eat. I shake my head. That piece of pizza I ate earlier is sitting heavily in my stomach and the waves of anxiety I'm feeling aren't helping matters.

"Stay cool, Jasmine," I mutter to myself. "You can do this. He'll be gone soon."

I gulp when I hear the prince ask for everyone's attention. The commanding tone in his voice sends shivers down my spine.

"Ladies and gentleman, allow me to introduce myself to you. I am Prince Oboroten, the founder and principal sponsor of the Riviera Musical Rodeo. I'm delighted to see all of this talent in one room and am looking forward to personally congratulating the three finalists who will be going on to the second round of the competition."

The rest of what he says is a blur to me. All I can think about is what will happen if the prince discovers the truth about who Whiskey and Bragi's fiddler really is.

****

The next few hours fly by. After successfully avoiding the prince during his welcome speech to the competing bands, I waited anxiously until it was Whiskey and Bragi's turn to perform. My stomach churned as we walked onto the stage, but the minute I tucked my violin into the crook of my neck and placed it under my chin, my nerves evaporated.

One of the songs Asger selected for us to play was a classic Dolly Parton tune. Asger made it his own with his distinctive gravely twang and his soulful guitar. J.B. on the bass and Raphael on the drums were the perfect complement, and I managed to not disgrace myself on the fiddle.

When we played the last note, I didn't want to leave the stage. It was a rush being up there, especially when the audience jumped to their feet cheering. This wasn't a reaction I normally experienced when performing with the Fjura Quartet.

Now we're sitting in the greenroom on one of the couches waiting for the rest of the bands to perform. The competition is stiff. We can see them on monitors positioned around the room. There's one band in particular I think will be hard to beat–Mrs. Moto & Co. They're from a small town in Florida. When they're not playing country music, they're out surfing, sailing, or wrestling alligators.

"You're sure you don't want anything to eat?" Raphael asks me. "They just put out some ribs and cornbread."

"No, I'm fine," I say. "But thank you."

"Well, I'm gonna grab some." J.B. points at Asger. "How about you? Want any?"

Asger says he's not hungry, then turns to me once Raphael and J.B. head off to load up their plates.

"I think our chances are good," he says to me. "And I don't just mean the competition."

"Huh?" I glance at Asger before looking back at the monitor. The band currently on stage just messed up. The lead singer froze, forgetting the lyrics. It's excruciating to watch and a good reminder that nerves can strike anyone at any time.

Asger taps my knee to get my attention. "I'm talking about us."

I snap my head in Asger's direction. "Us?"

"You and me. Put them together and you get us."

"I get how pronouns work," I say lightly.

Asger looks down at his cowboy boots, then he takes a deep breath and lifts his head. Staring at me intently, he says, "I'm not talking about grammar."

"Grammar might be an easier discussion," I say. "Unless you bring up things like present perfect tense or the Oxford comma. Then I might be a bit lost."

"I don't want to have an easy discussion." His blue eyes bore into me. "I want to have a 'put your cards on the table and bet on love' kind of discussion."

"That sounds like a lyric from a country song," I say, squirming on the couch. "How does the next line go? Something about milking the cows and baking biscuits in a cast-iron skillet?"

Asger bites back a smile. "Cows and biscuits?"

"Yeah, this is why I don't write country music tunes. I leave it to the professionals," I say, pointing at Asger. "Speaking of which, if we get through to the finals, the song you wrote is going to blow the judges' minds. It's beyond amazing."

"Not if. When." Asger shakes his head. "You're very evasive, by the way."

"How so?"

"Like this. Playing dumb. Changing the subject. Trying to distract me with flattery," Asger says firmly. "We're not high school kids anymore. We can have a frank discussion about how we feel about each other. We don't need to dance around the subject."

I fold my arms across my chest. "I hate to break it to you, but adults are just as much of idiots as high schoolers. Maybe even more so. Talking about this kind of stuff is hard."

Asger's expression softens. "Maybe this is a cultural thing. Danes are pretty direct."

"I don't know. There are Americans who are direct as well. Maybe not as many as in Denmark, but . . ." My voice trails off as I take Asger's hand in mine. As I rub my fingers gently across the back of his hand, I think about my next move.

Do I want to have this conversation? What happens if we do? Things will change. They would have to. But what would it change into? What do I even want? The last time I fell for a guy, it nearly destroyed me.

But this situation is different. Instead of a whirlwind romance with a guy I just met, Asger and I have known each other since high school. Granted, we only reconnected a couple of weeks ago, but the friendship we built while in the tenth grade means we're not starting from scratch. This man whose hand I'm holding–I know him. I get him. He knows me. He gets me.

"Jasmine," Asger says gently. "Do you want me to drop it?"

I let go of Asger's hand and run my fingers through

my hair. "I . . . um . . . no . . . I mean . . . you see . . . but we . . ."

J.B. and Raphael hurry toward us, disrupting my stream of spluttering nonsense. Raphael jams his cowboy hat on his head while J.B. motions to us. "Come on, we need to get on stage. They're about to announce the finalists."

I grab my violin case from the floor–there's no way I'm going to leave Joshua unattended in the greenroom–then rush after the guys. We're the last band on stage, which isn't a bad thing. I can stay hidden near the curtains while the emcee announces the finalists. What I'm going to do if he announces Whiskey and Bragi's name and we're thrust into the spotlight is another matter. I've gotta hope that this cowboy hat really does hide my face.

While the emcee prattles on about how hard it was for the judges to decide who is going to advance to the next round, I'm distracted by movement in the wings. I glance over, assuming it's going to be one of the stagehands, then frown when I see Terese.

It's like looking in a mirror–the same heavy eye makeup and hair worn down in loose curls. The only difference is in how we're dressed. I'm rocking the Viking cowboy look. She's dressed like one of the catering staff from the greenroom–black pants, black shirt, and a white bib apron.

I nudge J.B. As he swivels his head to look in the direction I'm pointing at, I ask in hushed tones, "What is she doing here?"

"Nothing good," he whispers back.

"It can't be a coincidence she's here," I say.

"No," J.B. agrees.

Terese makes an obscene gesture at us, then pivots on her heel and walks away.

I'm so stunned by Terese's sudden appearance that it's only when Asger starts making a whooping noise that I realize the emcee has announced Whiskey and Bragi's name. He slaps J.B. and Raphael on their backs, then pulls me into a quick hug. The emcee calls for us to join the other two finalists at the front of the stage. I hug my violin to the front of my body, hoping the top part of the case helps hide my face.

The next ten minutes are excruciating as the emcee talks to each band leader about their performance tonight, and what songs they're planning on singing during the finals. The prince is sitting in the front row. I'm convinced he's staring directly at me, trying to figure out how he knows me. Any minute now, he's going to leap to his feet and reveal me as an imposter.

When the emcee asks Asger to introduce the other members of Whiskey and Bragi, my stomach clenches. Will he stumble over my name, calling me Jasmine instead of Terese? I breathe a sigh of relief when Asger gets through the introductions without a hitch, then practically run off the stage as soon as the curtain drops.

Once I'm safely backstage, I breathe a sigh of relief. I set my violin case on the floor and slump against the wall as my adrenaline levels drop. I watch as the other bands file past, disappointment etched on most of their faces.

"There you are. I've been looking everywhere for you."

Asger is standing in front of me, his eyes shining with excitement, grinning from ear to ear. I don't think I've ever seen him so happy before. It's infectious. I feel myself smiling. I fling my arms around Asger and pull him into an embrace. As he lifts me up and spins me around, I start giggling at the absurdity of it all.

"What's so funny?" he whispers, his lips brushing against my ear.

"Never in a million years did I think I'd be dressed as a Viking cowboy in the middle of Monte Carlo," I say between fits of laughter.

Asger slowly sets me on my feet, then looks at me with such intense longing that my mouth goes dry. That's when it hits me. This is a man I can trust.

"Take your hat off," I say to him.

He furrows his brow. "Why?"

"Because I don't want it to get in the way." I fling my own hat on the ground, then once he's done the same, I snake my hands through his hair, pulling his face closer to mine. I leave a trail of fluttering, teasing kisses on both sides of his face, then press my lips against his, letting him know without any shadow of a doubt that he's *my* Viking cowboy.

When we come up for air, Asger shoots me a questioning look. I give him a shy smile. "That conversation you wanted to have? We're having it."

"Can the words wait for a little bit?" Asger asks. Then his lips find mine again.

We eventually break apart, but only because a stagehand interrupts us.

"Come on, let's go find J.B. and Raphael," Asger says as he grabs our hats off the floor.

I bend down to get my violin, then I gasp. "Joshua's gone!"

CHAPTER 9
THE MUSICAL DETECTIVES

"What do you mean Joshua is gone?" Asger asks, concern etched on his brow.

"I put my violin case there. Right there. Now it's gone." I point down at the floor, my voice getting increasingly high-pitched. "Someone stole Joshua."

"I'm sure your violin is around here someplace," Asger says as he searches the area. He pokes behind a stack of chairs, sound equipment, and the heavy drapes, but comes up empty-handed.

"Madame, monsieur, I'm sorry, but I must ask you to leave this area. We're locking up for the night," the stagehand who had interrupted us earlier says. "Please go collect your belongings from the greenroom."

"I *am* looking for my belongings," I snap.

Asger puts his arm around my shoulder. "Hey, easy. He's only doing his job."

Realizing that I've clenched my fists, I slowly relax my fingers, then smile sweetly at the stagehand. "Perhaps you can help us. Did you see anyone walk away from here with a violin case?"

The stagehand furrows his brow. "Of course."

I can feel my pulse pounding. Peering closely at the stagehand, I quickly ask, "Who? Who did you see? Can you describe them?"

"Which one?" he asks.

"What do you mean 'which one'?" I throw my hands in the air. "The person who stole my violin. What did they look like? Could you identify them in a line-up?"

The stagehand gives me a befuddled look. "Why would we line up violin players?"

"To identify the guilty party." I shake my head. How can this guy be so dense? Hasn't he ever seen a police procedural show? Read a mystery novel? Played Clue? "You point out who stole my violin, the police arrest them, and I get my violin back. Or do you folks do things differently in Monaco? Maybe put a classified in the paper politely asking the thief to leave the stolen goods on a bench at the park?"

The stagehand stares at me open-mouthed.

"Why don't you let me try?" Asger suggests. He turns to the stagehand. "What my friend is trying to find out is if you saw someone take *her* violin case."

"That's what I just asked," I mutter under my breath.

"I saw many people with violin cases walking around here tonight. But I wouldn't know if any of them were your friend's case. They all look similar." The stagehand smiles at Asger. "The music tonight was very interesting. I had never heard anyone play the violin like that before. What do you call it? Fingle?"

"Fiddle," Asger tells him. "So just to be clear, you didn't see anyone in the last ten minutes pick up a violin case from over by that wall and walk away with it."

The stagehand shakes his head. "No, I arrived here only a couple of minutes ago. I cleared my throat a couple of times to get your attention, but the two of you were, um, busy."

"Well, this has been a waste of time," I say. Then I remember seeing Terese in the wings earlier, glaring at me. "Did you see a woman who looks like me except, instead of a Viking cowboy outfit, she would have been wearing a catering uniform? Did you see anyone matching that description lurking around backstage just now? Maybe acting sneaky and holding a violin case?"

The stagehand denied noticing anyone that fit Terese's description, then insisted that we needed to leave. "I'm sorry that I can't help you. Perhaps if you check with lost and found in the morning, someone will have turned in your violin."

As he ushers us to the greenroom, Asger gives me a curious look. "Were you asking about Terese?"

I nod. "J.B. and I saw her earlier while we were waiting for them to announce the finalists."

"She was on stage?"

"No, Terese was in the wings, watching us. And she did not look happy to see me. She even flipped me off."

We halt our conversation when we reach the greenroom. The stagehand waits, presumably not trusting us to leave on our own accord. It doesn't take long to grab our stuff, especially me. I feel naked walking out of there with only a backpack and no violin.

Asger's phone buzzes as we're walking out. "J.B. and Raphael are heading to the Café de Formula 1 to have a celebratory drink. They're wondering where we are."

"I'm not in the mood to celebrate," I say as my eyes well up. "I'm sorry. You go."

"No, I want to hear more about Terese," he says. "And I'm not leaving you alone like this."

Asger places his guitar case on the ground as we sit on a bench outside the auditorium. It overlooks the Mediterranean Sea and, in normal circumstances, would feel very romantic. My eyes take in the moonlight reflecting off the water and a sailboat making port. I wish I could enjoy it, but the loss of

Joshua weighs heavily on me.

"So, tell me what happened with Terese," Asger says.

"There's not much to tell. If I hadn't looked over there, I might not have even noticed her."

"But she obviously noticed you. You said she flipped you off." Asger shakes his head. "Terese has always had a bit of a temper, but why take it out on you?"

"You got me. The woman is downright hostile toward me, for some unfathomable reason." I shrug. "*She* was the one who had quit Whiskey and Bragi, forcing me to step in at the last minute. It's not like I wanted to take over for her in the first place."

"Do you think that's what it is? She's jealous that you're in the band now?"

An idea dawns on me. "Maybe it's not about me *personally*."

"Well, how could it be? She doesn't even know you."

I twist on the bench to face Asger. "Exactly. Maybe she's upset that you were able to replace her. Maybe she didn't want Whiskey and Bragi to compete in the Riviera Musical Rodeo in the first place."

He furrows his brow. "Are you saying she wanted us to drop out?"

"It's a possible explanation," I say. "It fits with what happened at the prince's birthday party."

"You didn't mention anything about the birthday

party to me."

"We didn't want to worry you."

Asger folds his arms across his chest. "We?"

"J.B. and me," I say. "He and Terese were both working the party."

"Okay." Asger relaxes slightly. "What happened?"

"Terese insulted classical music and told me she didn't think I could pull off playing the fiddle in your band."

"Why do I feel like there's more to the story?"

I take off my cowboy hat, wincing as one of the Viking horns attached on the sides pokes me. "Well, she warned me to stay on her good side, otherwise she'd tell the competition organizers I'm impersonating her."

"But she didn't do that. We're still in the competition." Asger groans. "You don't think she's going to wait until the finals to rat us out, do you?"

"I'm not sure what she's going to do." I stare off into the water for a few minutes, then say, "There's another possibility. What if she made sure to get a job at the auditorium tonight, not so that she could rat us out to the competition organizers, but so that she could steal my violin?"

Asger runs his hands through his hair. "That doesn't make sense. She has a violin of her own."

"But she doesn't have an Avestruz. When she found out that I owned one, she was very interested. But maybe she wasn't interested in my violin for herself, though. She said she could hook me up with a buyer for it if I wanted to sell it." I lean forward. "What if she decided to cut me out of the picture, steal my violin, and sell it herself? Maybe it was all about the money."

"So, now you're saying she doesn't care if you perform with Whiskey and Bragi."

"No, I definitely think she cares. Why it bothers her, that's still a mystery." I press my lips together as yet another idea rushes into my mind. "Unless she's jealous of you and me. Were the two of you an item?"

"What?" Asger's eyes widen. "No. Never. No way."

I study him for a moment. His reaction seems genuine. But you can't deny that Terese and I have similar looks. Maybe Asger has a type. When his relationship with Terese ended and I came along on the scene, I was the perfect replacement.

"Terese has been going out with the same guy for years," Asger says, interrupting my thoughts. "Even if she wasn't, I would have zero interest in her. She's not my type."

When I point out our physical similarities, Asger snorts. "The resemblance is slight. Anyone that knows the two of you could tell the difference."

I frown. "Yet you have me out there on stage pretending to be her?"

"That was your idea, if you'll recall," he says a bit snippily.

"You were happy to say yes," I point out.

Asger closes his eyes and rubs his temples. When he looks back at me, his brow is creased. "Do you see what's happening here? Terese is turning the two of us against each other. You're right. I shouldn't have agreed to let you fill in for Terese. It wasn't fair to you. Look what's happened as a result–your violin is gone."

"You're right. We're letting her win." I narrow my eyes. "And she's not going to win. I'm going to get my violin back no matter what."

"And I'm going to help you," Asger says. "But we need a plan. If we confront Terese, she'll just deny it."

"What about the police? Shouldn't we call them?"

Asger thinks about this for a moment, then shakes his head. "Terese is a clever girl. She'll have covered her tracks. We don't have any proof she stole it. It would just be our word against hers."

I let out a sigh. "You're right."

"Come on. Let's get you home." Asger pulls me to my feet. "I think we should come at this with fresh eyes tomorrow."

I feel electric sparks between us as Asger slowly caresses my hands. I'm so tempted to pull him toward me and finish what we started earlier backstage. Instead, I abruptly pull away.

Asger looks at me with a wounded expression in his eyes. "What's wrong?"

"The reason this happened is because we got carried away with each other," I say slowly. "Joshua is gone because I got distracted. It was a mistake. A big mistake. And it's never going to happen again."

* * *

The next morning, everyone gathers at Sebastien's villa for a late brunch. And by everyone, I mean the members of the Fjura Quartet *and* the guys in Whiskey and Bragi. This should have been a fun occasion–the two groups meeting for the first time and celebrating the fact that Asger and his band got through to the finals of the Riviera Musical Rodeo. But fun, it most certainly is not.

Okay, some of that is down to me. Maybe a lot of it. I'm devastated by the theft of Joshua, and I'm taking it out on Asger and anyone else within a five-mile radius. But mostly Asger. If we hadn't gotten swept away in the heat of the moment, I would still have my violin. Bad things happen when you kiss a guy, like being taken in by a scam artist or losing your most precious possession, your Avestruz violin.

But there's also another issue which concerns both groups–my complete and utter lack of a violin. When you're a violinist or a fiddler or whatever you want to call yourself, you kind of need a violin. The quartet has a concert tonight. If I turn up with a banjo and tuck it under my chin, I don't think people are going to be fooled.

You'd think finding an instrument I could rent for

the night would be a piece of cake. But guess what? There seems to be an inexplicable shortage of violins in the area. Something to do with an orchestra camp in Germany with an insatiable need for all the available violins in Europe.

Borrowing a violin from a professional musician in the area proved impossible as well. Word was out that my violin had been stolen. No one wanted to risk loaning theirs to me for fear that they'd never see it again.

So that was the Fjura Quartet's immediate concern. What was I going to play at the concert tonight? A banjo was beginning to look like the best option.

Whiskey and Bragi's focus was a little less immediate, but a lot more consequential. I'm convinced it would be bad luck if I play anything other than Joshua at the Riviera Musical Rodeo. The finals were less than a week away. Would we be able to track my violin down by then?

Grace taps me on my shoulder, interrupting me from my obsessive thoughts about my missing violin. "Jasmine, can you carry the orange juice in?"

I'm sitting on a stool in the kitchen staring into my water glass while Grace puts the finishing touches on food. The others are hanging out in the music room. Grace is planning on serving a casual buffet style meal with miniature quiches, freshly baked pastries and bread, fruit salad, and an assortment of cold cuts and cheeses.

She hands me the container of juice, then picks up a tray laden with goodies. When he sees us enter the music room, Pedro rushes over to take the tray from Grace. She shoos him away, telling him to get some glasses and napkins.

"You know he likes you, don't you," I say to Grace as I set the orange juice down on the makeshift buffet table that's been set up by the piano.

Grace gives me a funny look. "What do you mean?"

"He's smitten with you." I smile as I use the old-fashioned term. Then my smile fades as I remember the last time I had said it, when I called my friend Olivia from the casino. Had that only been a little over two weeks ago? I had just run into Asger, stunned to discover the former foreign exchange student was working as a waiter in Monaco. In the span of the time since then, we'd rekindled our old friendship, then made the fateful mistake of thinking it could be more than that.

"He's not smitten with me." Grace shakes her head. "I think you're projecting. You're the one who is smitten. Smitten with Asger."

"I was," I say matter-of-factly. "Now I've come to my senses."

Pedro returns with the glasses and napkins, followed by the others, each one carrying a tray of food, basket of bread, or bowl of fruit. Once everything is arranged on the table, everyone fixes a plate for themselves, then heads over to the seating area.

As I settle down on the couch next to J.B., he squeezes my shoulder. "How are you holding up?"

"Not great," I say. "I really appreciate everything you've all done trying to find me a replacement violin for tonight."

"Don't worry. We'll keep trying." J.B. hesitates, then says in an undertone, "You seem to be avoiding Asger."

"Yeah, I know." I toy with the piece of bread on my plate. "It's complicated."

J.B. lets it go, turning to chat with Grace about whether she puts cayenne pepper in her quiche. Asger is at the other end of the seating area, having an animated discussion with Pedro, Sebastien, and Raphael about whether Ted Lasso is the best soccer coach the world has ever seen. I sit quietly, so lost in thought that I don't even notice what I'm eating.

As I set my empty plate on the coffee table, Pedro whistles to get everyone's attention. Once there's silence in the room, he says, "Now that everyone has finished the delicious food Grace prepared for us, I'd like to call this meeting to order."

I furrow my brow. The others look confused as well. "What meeting?" I ask.

"This is the first official meeting of the Musical Detectives Agency," Pedro says solemnly.

Pedro is sitting up straight with a notebook and

pen in hand, and his expression is deadly serious. Even his usually unruly hair seems to have taken notice of this change in his persona, from adorably goofy to professionally somber. Instead of sticking out at weird angles, it's smooth and controlled.

He looks around to make sure everyone is paying attention, then continues, "We're going to investigate the crime, nab the perpetrator, and find your violin."

Grace bursts out laughing. "Someone has been watching too many detective shows."

Noticing how deflated the poor guy looks, I quickly jump in. "Thank you, Pedro. If there's one thing this whole event has shown me is what good friends I have, both old and new. I'll take any help I can get in finding Joshua."

"I'm sorry. I shouldn't have teased you." Grace puts her hands to her chest in a mea culpa gesture. "Please, go ahead."

"Hmm . . . the Musical Detectives Agency." J.B. rubs his chin. "I like the sound of that."

"We could get badges in the shape of magnifying glasses with our names on them," Pedro says, his good humor restored.

Sebastien chuckles. "Let's do it."

The others nod, then Raphael asks, "Where do we start? What's our plan?"

I look over at Asger, making eye contact with him for the first time this morning. Realizing that I've been unfair to him, I give him a small smile. Even though I think pursuing a romantic relationship with Asger is a bad idea, he's still my friend. A friend I don't want to lose.

Asger clears his throat. "We've filled you in already about Terese's threatening remarks and showing up at the competition. It's pretty obvious that she stole Jasmine's violin when we were, um, you know . . ."

"Distracted," I suggest.

He gives me a grateful look. "Yes, Terese took the violin when Jasmine and I were distracted. We don't have any evidence that Terese stole the violin and I think it's safe to say that Terese would have been too smart to stash the violin at her apartment. Ideally, we'd get Terese to confess, then she'd willingly give the violin back, but I don't think that's going to happen."

Pedro jots something down in his notebook, then says, "I think we need to talk with Terese's associates and see if they have any information about where the violin is."

"What associates?" Asger asks. "She doesn't seem to have many close friends."

"We should start with her boyfriend," Raphael says. "And the woman she shares an apartment with."

"I know her roommate," J.B. says. "I've done catering jobs with her before."

"Can you speak with her this afternoon?" Pedro asks.

J.B. nods, then Asger mentions that he's met

Terese's boyfriend a few times. "We both like Formula 1. Why don't I see if I can track him down today?"

"While you guys are doing that, I'll make some more phone calls and see if I can find a loaner violin for Jasmine," Sebastien says.

We chat for a few more minutes about the investigation, then Grace and Raphael start to clear away the plates. J.B. suggests we all meet back here in the afternoon to report in. As Asger gets up from his chair, I tell him that I need to grab my purse.

"Why do you need your purse?" he asks.

"My gut is telling me Terese's boyfriend is the key," I say. "You don't think I'd let you go see him without me, do you?"

CHAPTER 10
TURD FACE

As Asger and I get ready to head to Terese's boyfriend's place, Sebastien offers to loan us one of his cars. "Which one do you want? The Jaguar or the Mercedes?"

"We can take a taxi or the bus," I say.

Sebastien shakes his head. "It's already one-thirty. If you don't find the boyfriend . . . what's his name?"

"Nico," Asger says.

"Anyway, if you don't find Nico at his apartment, you might have to try to track him down in his other usual haunts. That could take some time and our recital is at six. You'll be able to get around quicker if you drive."

My eyes widen. "But I haven't driven a car in years."

"Oh, I wasn't planning on handing the keys to

you," Sebastien says with a chuckle. He turns to Asger. "I also have a Range Rover and an Aston Martin. Take your pick."

Asger looks like a little kid who has been let loose in a candy shop. "What kind of Aston Martin?"

"Have you ever seen *Her Majesty's Secret Service*?" Sebastien asks. "It's like the one in that."

"Ooh, a James Bond car." Asger turns to me, a huge grin on his face. "That sounds perfect, don't you think? We are going on on a spy mission after all."

I put my hand on Asger's arm. "That's the movie where James Bond gets married and his wife is killed. Kind of feels like bad luck. Besides, we're detectives, not spies."

"What's the difference?" Asger asks.

"Good question." I consider this for a moment, then say, "Spies like James Bond go undercover and gather intelligence. Detectives investigate crimes and uncover clues. They probably also drive sensible cars."

Asger arches an eyebrow. "You mean boring cars. But you have a point. If we turn up in Nico's neighborhood driving one of Sebastien's flashy cars, it'll raise a lot of questions."

"I do have a boring car you can borrow." Sebastien grabs a set of keys from a drawer in the kitchen, then hands them to Asger. "These are for a VW Golf which the housekeeper uses to run errands."

It takes a bit of persuasion, but Asger finally gives

up his hopes of driving a James Bond Aston Martin. As we pull out of the garage, I try to console Asger. "It might not be a sporty ride, but at least it's red."

Asger shifts the car into gear, then flashes me a grin. "The hatchback is what makes it."

We make our way through Monte Carlo, driving along the road which runs along the coastline. The beaches we pass are so tempting. What I wouldn't give to go swimming in the crystal blue waters, followed by nestling on a blanket, enjoying a picnic of crusty French bread, cheese, and olives. Asger and I would wrap our arms around each other, our toes dug into the sand, and watch the sunset. And there'd be kissing. Lots and lots of kissing.

When Asger turns the car away from the water, I let out a deep sigh. I need to control my imagination. Thinking about the way it felt when Asger's lips were pressed against mine last night is not helpful.

Mistaking my reaction for concern, Asger pats my hand. "Don't worry, we'll find Joshua."

I chew on my bottom lip. "What's Nico like?"

"I've only met him a few times. He's not a very talkative guy. I don't know much about him other than the fact that he works construction, and he loves motorsports. He picks up odd jobs at the Formula 1 race each year." Asger turns the VW Golf onto a busy road and we wind our way through the mountainous terrain. "What I can tell you is that he is not a fan of country music. Heavy metal is more his thing."

"To be fair, I wasn't exactly a country music fan either until I started playing with your band." I smile at Asger. "But it's growing on me."

"Sounds like a girl who needs her own Dolly Parton t-shirt," he says, pointing down at his chest. He's wearing yet another shirt with the blonde country music legend on it. I didn't dare tell him that you can buy cake mix back in the States with Dolly's face on it. He'd be having me ship him cartons and cartons of it over to him.

I roll my eyes. "Exactly how many Dolly t-shirts do you own?"

"Not nearly enough."

We enter a tunnel, and I hold my breath for good luck. Turns out there are several more tunnels to go through along our route, some so long that I'm gasping for air as we exit them. It gives me a chance to wish for all sorts of things: finding my violin, Whiskey and Bragi winning the Riviera Musical Rodeo, and figuring out how to get back into the friends-only zone with Asger.

"I didn't realize Nico lived so far away," I say when Asger eventually parks the car in front of a building which houses a travel agency and florist on the bottom floor and apartments on the upper floors. "I'm glad we drove."

As we get out of the car, Asger says, "Welcome to Italy."

"Seriously?" I look around me, realizing that the

signs are now in Italian and not French. "It blows my mind that we can travel from Monaco to France and Italy like that," I say, snapping my fingers.

Asger studies the buzzers next to the glass door, then smacks his forehead. "I can't remember Nico's last name, let alone what apartment number is his. I was only here once before when J.B. dropped Terese off after a gig."

"One way to find out." I press each button in turn. When no one responds, I start cycling through the buttons again. After the third try, a voice speaking in rapid-fire Italian comes out of the intercom.

I gesture at Asger, but he shakes his head. "I don't speak Italian."

We try asking about Nico in English, but that only causes the disembodied voice to speak more quickly and more loudly in Italian. French doesn't do us any good either. The man sounds increasingly agitated. Finally, the voice goes silent. I go to press the button again, but Asger stops me.

"I don't think it's going to help," he says. "That last bit of Italian I understood. He basically told us to get lost."

"I have a feeling he didn't put it quite as politely as that."

We both slump down on the stoop and reassess our plan. Coming here in the hope that Nico would be home on a Sunday afternoon wasn't all that well thought through. Being a detective was harder than I anticipated.

"Should we try the bars and cafés around here and see if anyone knows where Nico is?" I suggest.

"Let's give it a few minutes. Maybe he popped out to the shop for something and he'll be back soon." Asger looks at me out of the corner of his eye. "Besides, it will give us a chance to talk about what happened last night."

"Honestly, I don't want to talk about it anymore." I squeeze my hands together. "I've rehashed how Joshua was stolen too many times already today."

After a beat, Asger says, "I meant the other thing that happened."

"Oh . . . that thing."

"Yeah, that thing."

Neither of us says anything for the longest time. Then we both speak at once. "It shouldn't have happened," I say while Asger says, "I'm glad it happened."

There's more silence, even more uncomfortable than before. A few cars pass by and I will one of them to stop, letting Nico out so that we have something else to focus our attention on. Finally, I decide it's better to get it over with. We aren't getting back to the friends-only zone otherwise.

"It's not you, it's me." I cringe as the words trip off my tongue. Maybe there are some other ridiculous cliches I can trot out so I can look like even more of an idiot.

I'm still getting over my ex. Not true. I'm angry about losing my life savings and I feel like a fool for having married that jerk, but I'm so glad he's out of my life. Not a chance I'd ever get back with him.

We want different things out of life. Kind of true. Asger loves country music. I love classical. He wears crazy Viking cowboy costumes when performing. I wear understated dresses. He wants to make it big, touring around the world with his band. I want to keep playing with our quartet, maybe even become a solo violinist like Joshua Bell one day. Can you imagine being in demand by all the major orchestras? But there's more to life than our careers, right? That's what I always tell my friend Olivia. What else does Asger want from life? What do I want?

Too many deep questions there. I quickly shift my thoughts back to those classic cliche break-up lines. *You deserve better.* Hmm. Is this one true or not? I pride myself on not being too insecure about myself. I'm worthy of a decent guy. Could Asger do better than me? Maybe that's the wrong question. Maybe I'm not the right woman for him, not because there's someone out there better than me, but because we're not the right fit for each other.

What else do people say when they're ending things? Not that we're really ending things. Things barely even got started. One impetuous make-out session backstage hardly constitutes a relationship.

There's always the classic line, *You're a great guy.* True. So true. Asger really is a great guy. He loves music. He makes me laugh. He's kind. He'd do anything for me. And man, can that guy kiss. So why don't I want to be with him? I'm not sure I know the answer. I'm not sure I want to know the answer. All I do know is that my gut is telling me that Asger and I shouldn't be together.

I take a deep breath. But as I'm about to tell Asger that we can still be friends, he points at a man with shaggy brown hair wearing an Iron Maiden t-shirt walking toward us.

"That's Nico," Asger says as he gets to his feet. "We're going to speak with him about your violin. But just so we're clear, we're not done talking about you and me. Not by a longshot."

* * *

Nico scowls as he approaches us. "If you're looking for Terese, she's not here," he says to Asger.

"No, I was actually looking for you. We were in the neighborhood and I remembered that you lived around here," Asger says, holding out his hand.

As Nico and Asger shake, I'm fascinated by how lifelike the tattoos on Nico's arms are. Logically, I know it's only ink pigments under the skin, but it still gives me the creeps. I have this sudden, unrealistic fear that one of the snakes is going to come to life, slither off Nico's skin and onto Asger's, sinking its fangs into him and injecting him with poison.

I grab the hem of Asger's Dolly Parton t-shirt and pull him back. Nico stares at me, his eyes cold and hard. Then he turns back to Asger. "This your girlfriend?"

Asger gives me a wry smile, as if daring me to answer. So I do. Just not in the way he expects.

"Yes, I'm his girlfriend," I say.

Ridiculous, I know. As if claiming Asger as mine can protect him from snake tattoos coming to life and killing him with their imaginary poison. This is what happens when I don't get any sleep.

"I hope she treats you better than Terese treated me," Nico says to Asger.

"Why? What did Terese do?" I ask.

Nico ignores me, fixing his beady eyes on Asger. "What did you want to see me about, anyway?"

"I heard about some possible work at next year's Grand Prix and thought about you," Asger says.

"Oh, yeah? What kind of work?"

"At one of the hospitality tents. You'd be close to the action on the track."

Nico frowns. "Is it under the table?"

"Um, I'm not sure," Asger says. "Maybe?"

"Nope, no way." Nico holds up his hands. "I don't need any more trouble from the police."

I press my lips together. Of course, he's had run-ins with the law before. No surprise there. Just look at him.

"No worries." Asger shrugs. "Maybe Terese might be interested?"

"How would I know?" Nico folds his arms across his chest. "Ask her yourself."

"Are you expecting her?" I ask.

"If I don't ever see her again, that will be soon enough," Nico says before spitting on the ground.

I furrow my brow. "Did you two break up?"

"Yeah. After what she pulled yesterday, I finally came to my senses." Nico glares at me for a long moment, then his face crumples. He struggles to gain his composure, wiping away a tear from his eyes.

"What happened?" I ask gently.

"She was using me," Nico says, his breath hitching. "When we first started dating, I told her I had gone straight. But she'd give me some sob story after another. Each and every time, I'd cave. I was in love with her, you know."

I take a tentative step forward and give him a 'there, there' pat on the arm, being careful to avoid touching any of his snake tattoos. The tears streaming down Nico's face made him seem harmless now, but I'm still wary of the creatures on his skin.

"Why don't you come sit down?" I guide Nico over to the stoop. "It might help to talk about it."

"What the heck?" Asger mouths to me.

I shake my head, confused as he is about Nico's

breakdown. Sitting next to the sobbing man, I tentatively say, "Sounds like she conned you. That happened to me, too."

Nico turns to me. "It did?"

"Uh-huh." I'm hoping to leave it there, but Nico gives me such a pitiful look that I proceed to spill my guts against my better judgment. "I met this guy last year when I was living in San Francisco. It was at a black tie fundraiser for the Conservatory of Music. We got to talking, and he told me he was Joshua Bell's personal assistant."

"Who is Joshua Bell?" Nico asks.

I give him an incredulous look. "Only the most brilliant violinist of our time."

"If you say so," Nico says. "Terese probably knows who he is."

"I'll bet she does," I say bitterly, thinking about how she stole my violin. The one I named after the one and only Joshua Bell. Softening my expression, I continue with my story. "Anyway, this guy–"

Asger interrupts. "What's his name?"

"It doesn't matter." I shake my head. "Let's just call him Turd Face, okay? As I was saying, Turd Face and I ended up sitting in the corner of the room talking about classical music and Joshua Bell all night. Have you ever had one of those moments where you meet someone and you're utterly captivated? Hours fly by and you don't even realize it."

"Sounds like me and Terese. It was love at first

sight." Nico grimaces. "At least, I thought it was. Now, I know better."

"Same thing happened to me," I say. "I was convinced Turd Face was my soulmate. The fact that he was Joshua Bell's personal assistant seemed like a sign from the universe. I fell so hard. It's embarrassing."

Asger is staring at me intently. I can't read his expression. Is he angry? Jealous? Feeling sorry for me? I mentally shake myself, then turn back to Nico. "After the reception was over, Turd Face suggested we go for a nightcap. It didn't take much convincing, to be honest. I wasn't ready to say good night. I didn't want to let him out of my sight. It was like I was intoxicated despite the fact that I had only had one glass of wine that night."

"Drunk on love," Nico mutters. "The hangover from that is way worse than if you had been drinking booze instead."

"Yeah, don't I know it." I toy with the bracelet on my wrist, not sure I want to share the next part of the story. I hem and haw for a few moments, then just go for it. This is the first time I've ever really talked about what happened in detail. It feels kind of cathartic. "So, we get a taxi to take us to the swanky bar with amazing views of the Golden Gate Bridge. When we get there, Turd Face makes like he's going to pay the taxi fare. He reaches into his pocket, then his face turns bright red."

"Let me guess. Turd Face 'forgot' his wallet," Asger says dryly, making air quotes.

"Yep." I arch an eyebrow. "Apparently, he had been rushing around on a call with Joshua before he left for the reception and completely forgot to grab his wallet. He looked so embarrassed. I believed him. I paid for the taxi, then we stopped at an ATM so I could get some cash out to loan to Turd Face. Little did I realize, he was staring over my shoulder when I entered my PIN number."

That was a half-truth. Turd Face wasn't staring over my shoulder. He was actually kissing my neck when I was at the ATM, giving him a prime viewing spot when I typed in my four digit code on the keypad. I was so distracted at the time, I didn't even think about it. But Asger doesn't need to know all the details of what happened, does he?

"I don't like where this story is going," Asger says.

"You and me both," I say.

Nico is leaning forward, hanging on my every word. I have a feeling what happened between him and Terese pales in comparison to my ill-fated hookup with Turd Face.

"We had a nice time at the bar. He ordered some really nice champagne and told me more stories about Joshua Bell. I was so caught up in it all that time slipped away again. Before you know it, they're telling us the place is closing."

"Naturally, you pay the check," Asger says.

"Despite the fact that you loaned him cash earlier."

I sigh. "That's not the worst of it. He told me I looked too comfortable sitting where I was, so he took my credit card up to the bar to settle the tab. When he came back to the table, he grabbed my purse and pretended like he slipped the card back in it, but he really pocketed it."

Asger grits his teeth. "You need to tell me Turd Face's real name. I want to have a word with him."

I smile at him. "That's sweet, but unnecessary."

"What happened next?" Nico asks eagerly.

I spread my hands in the air. "Long story short, Turd Face got a hold of the rest of my bank details and he cleaned me out. All in the matter of forty-eight hours."

Nico's jaw drops. Then he says something angrily in Italian while repeatedly smacking his fist into his hand. "Where is this Turd Face?"

Asger joins in. "Yeah, tell us where Turd Face is."

I know it shouldn't, but it feels good that two guys, one of whom I hadn't met before today, want to extract some sort of vengeance on my behalf. "I don't know where he is, honestly. But anyway, the laugh is on him . . . kind of."

"How so?" Asger asks.

"Someone had pointed me out to Turd Face at the reception, mistaking me for a rich socialite. Little did Turd Face know that I was only there that night because I got a free ticket. He thought he was going to milk me for my vast fortune. But when he logged into my banking account and saw how much I was really worth, well, let's just say it wasn't a lot. I mean, it was a lot to me. It was all I had. But it certainly wasn't the millions he had been expecting."

Asger shakes his head. "He wasn't really Joshua Bell's personal assistant, was he?"

"Nope, all part of his con game." I press my hands to my face. "Taking my money wasn't the worst part of it, though."

"Sounds pretty bad to me," Nico says. "What could be worse than that?"

I look down at the pavement, then say quietly, "I married him."

CHAPTER 11
CONFUSING METRIC TALK

After sharing the fact that I had been married to Turd Face, I continue to stare at the pavement for the longest time, hoping a black hole will form underneath my feet and suck me into a parallel universe where my alternate self never met Turd Face.

When I look back up, Asger is staring at me, jaw slack, eyes wide. "You look like a stunned mullet," I say to him.

"You were married?" He glances down at my left hand, as though looking for a ring. "Are you still married?"

"No. Technically, I was never really married. The whole thing was annulled. One of those elope to Las Vegas, realize what you've done, and get it undone as quickly as you can."

Asger runs his hands through his hair. "Why didn't you tell me?"

I make a twirling motion in the air with my finger, then point at myself. "Did you miss that whole embarrassing story I just shared? It's not something I'm proud of."

Nico looks back and forth between Asger and me. "How long have you two been going out?"

For some reason, this sets me off in fits of giggles. A smile creeps across Asger's face, then he starts roaring with laughter. When we finally gain control of ourselves, Nico asks if we want to come upstairs to his place for a beer.

That's when I remember why we're here–not to make impromptu confessions about my past love life, but to find my violin. I glance at my phone. It's already after three and we haven't even gotten any information from Nico about Terese.

"We can't right now. But definitely some other time," Asger says to Nico. "Hey, do you mind if we ask you a couple of questions about Terese?"

Nico scowls. "I'd rather not talk about her."

"It's actually about Joshua Bell," I say.

"Joshua?" Nico furrows his brow. "You mean the guy Turd Face pretended to be a personal assistant for? What does Terese have to do with Joshua or Turd Face?"

"Sorry. It's confusing," I say. "Joshua is actually the name of my violin."

"I thought Joshua was a violinist," Nico says.

I nod. "He is. He's an amazing violinist. The best violinist of our time. That's why I named my violin after him."

"That's a little weird," Nico says slowly.

"Everything about this situation is weird," I admit. "Anyhoo, let me cut to the chase. Terese took Joshua."

Nico cocks his head to one side. "The violinist or the violin?"

"The violin." I give Nico a quizzical look. "Has Terese kidnapped a person before?"

"Not as far as I know." Nico shrugs. "But if there was enough money involved, I wouldn't put it past her."

"That's a scary thought," Asger says. "If I had any idea how ruthless she was, I would have never asked her to join Whiskey and Bragi."

"Don't take it personally," Nico says to Asger. "She can charm the socks off a snake if she puts her mind to it."

"Wow, your English is really good. I don't think most non-native speakers would know an expression like that." I glance down at Nico's arms. "You do have a thing for snakes, don't you?"

"My mom is Canadian." He rubs his tattoos. "These are the only snakes I can have. I'm allergic to the real ones."

Asger steers us back to the topic of Terese. "When's the last time you saw her?"

"Last night," Nico says. "She showed up around eleven and asked if she could crash at my place. Something about a fight with her roommate."

I grip Nico's arm. "Did she have a violin with her?"

"Not sure," he says. "I buzzed her up, then went into the kitchen to get some water so I didn't see her when she came into the apartment. If she had the violin with her, she could have shoved it into the coat closet. But even if I had seen her with a violin, I probably would have assumed it was her own. She used to practice at my place."

I furrow my brow. "Really? I thought you hated the fact that she played the fiddle. That's why she quit Whiskey and Bragi."

"I didn't have anything to do with that. She knew I didn't like country music, but I thought it was cool that she played a musical instrument." Nico looks off into the distance. "That was one of the things that first attracted me to her."

Realizing I'm still holding onto Nico's arm, I quickly let go. Creeped out by the fact that I touched his snake tattoos, I rub my hands on my pants. "So what happened after Terese got here?" I ask.

"She picked a fight with me about something stupid." Nico narrows his eyes.

"Then we made up. I thought everything was fine, then this morning she told me that she needed my help with a job."

"You mean a catering job?" Asger asks.

"No, Terese said she needed me to deliver something. I knew right away it wasn't on the up and up. When I refused, she got angry. She screamed and stomped around the apartment, then she tried to turn the charm on and convince me to do her a favor." Nico exhales slowly. "I hate to admit it, but when she told me how much her client was going to pay her for what she needed delivered, I was tempted."

I slap my thighs. "She had to be talking about Joshua. He would be worth a lot to the right buyer."

"Did she say who the buyer was?" Asger asks.

Nico shakes his head. "All I know is that it was a guy. She's supposed to meet him at a private party tomorrow night and hand off the goods."

"Why did Terese want you to go in her place?" I ask.

"On the off chance that whoever she robbed was onto her."

"You mean me," I spit out. "And we are on to her. Where's this party taking place?"

"Got me." Nico presses his lips together. "When I refused to cooperate, she stormed out of the apartment. I haven't heard from her since. Come to think of it, she grabbed something from the coat closet before she left. Maybe it was your violin."

I clench my fists and let out a frustrated groan. "Now, what are we supposed to do? How are we going to figure out where this party is?"

Asger is pacing back and forth on the sidewalk,

looking equally upset. "This is all my fault," he mutters. "If I hadn't asked Terese to join Whiskey and Bragi in the first place, she would have never been in a position to meet you and steal your violin."

"Hey, it's not your fault." I jump to my feet and pull Asger into an embrace. "Besides, maybe we should be thanking Terese."

"Thanking Terese?" Asger pulls back, resting his hands on my shoulders. "Are you nuts? The woman stole your most prized possession."

"Yes, but if she didn't quit the band, then you and I wouldn't have spent so much time together over the past week," I say simply.

A smile plays across his lips as he traces his fingers along my cheek. "Weren't you the one who blamed what happened backstage for Joshua being stolen? If I remember correctly, you said something about us getting carried away and being distracted."

"You are very distracting." I stare into Asger's blue eyes, then tilt my head to the side as his fingers slide down my neck. "Very, very distracting."

When Nico clears his throat, I remember that we're standing on a sidewalk in front of his apartment building. My face grows warm. Stepping back from Asger, I shove my hands in my pockets and give Nico an embarrassed look.

"For what it's worth, you two seem good together," Nico says wistfully. "I hope you have better luck than Terese and I did."

As Asger pats Nico on the shoulder and assures him that the right girl is out there for him, I check my phone.

"Hey, we have to go," I tell Asger. "Pedro texted. He said J.B. just got back to Sebastien's villa."

"Did he say what happened with Terese's roommate?" Asger asks.

"Nope." I reread the text and roll my eyes. "According to Pedro, all official reports can only be delivered in person."

* * *

"Whoa, slow down," I say to Asger as he passes the car in front of us.

"Relax. I'm barely going ninety," he says to me. "You want to get back to Sebastien's place as soon as possible and hear what J.B. found out from Terese's roommate, don't you?"

I squeeze my eyes shut. "Ninety miles an hour? Are you crazy? This is a VW Golf, not a Formula 1 race car."

Asger chuckles. "Ninety *kilometers* an hour, not miles."

"Don't try to confuse me with your metric talk," I say. "You're still going too fast."

"Do you want to take the wheel?" he asks with a teasing tone in his voice. "Just say the word and I'll pull over."

I open my eyes and glare at Asger. "You know I can't drive."

"You drove in high school," he says. "So I know you *can* drive."

"Fine. I *can* drive," I say. "But it's something I'd rather avoid doing if I can help it."

He glances over at me. "Why's that?"

"Some guy side-swiped me a few years ago on the highway. I spun out of control and ended up in a ditch. Fortunately, I was fine, but my car was totaled." I fiddle with the shoulder strap of my seatbelt. "I've been a nervous driver ever since then. Instead of buying a new car with the insurance payout, I put it into my savings account and used public transportation and taxis instead."

Asger reaches over and squeezes my hand. "Maybe when this is all over, we should borrow a car from Sebastien again, get you back on the road, and build your confidence back up."

"Hey buddy, ten and two," I say.

"Ten and two?"

"Your hands. Put both your hands on the wheel. You know, the ten and two o'clock position."

"If I have both hands on the wheel, how do I shift gears?"

I shake my head. "If we do practice my driving, and that's a big if, we'll need to do it in an automatic. I haven't driven a stick shift since high school."

"Stick shift is so much better," Asger says. "You

have better control."

I breathe a sigh of relief when we pull onto the city streets in Monte Carlo and Asger is forced to slow down. My nerves are already on edge trying to track Terese and my violin down. The speeding through traffic to get here didn't help. But Asger is right. We have less than an hour before I need to get ready for the Fjura Quartet's recital–that is assuming Sebastien has been able to track down a violin for me. And we still need to meet with the rest of the Musical Detectives and figure out next steps in finding Joshua.

After parking the VW in the garage, we rush upstairs to the music room. The others are already there. Pedro is standing in front of a whiteboard by the seating area, explaining something to Raphael and Sebastien. Grace is sitting next to J.B. on the piano bench. watching him play a tune that sounds like a Bach prelude with a rockabilly twist. It's odd, to say the least. Good, but odd.

When Sebastien spots us, a grin spreads across his face. He points at the coffee table where a violin case is lying. "Good news. I found you a violin."

I feel a surge of hope coursing through my body. Could this be Joshua? But when I reach down to open the clasps of the case and see the instrument inside, my heart sinks. Instead of an exquisite Avestruz with its trademark kangaroo and koala engravings on the front, I'm confronted with a violin that's seen better days.

I pick it up and examine it. There are patches where varnish has been reapplied, the bridge looks loose, and there's a small open seam where the back of the violin meets the side.

"Sorry, it's not what you're used to," Sebastien says to me. "But at least you can play with the quartet tonight."

"It's okay." My eyes well up with tears as I tuck the violin under my chin. It feels so wrong to hold anything other than Joshua like this. "I appreciate it. I really do."

As I place the violin back in its case, Pedro motions for everyone to join him. "We don't have much time for our field investigators' reports."

"Field investigators?" J.B. smiles. "I like the sound of that. Can we put that on our badges?"

"Certainly," Pedro says, jotting down the suggestion in his notebook.

"I don't know why we couldn't share what we found out over the phone," I say.

"Your phones could be tapped," Pedro says seriously. "Sebastien has assured me that this room is free of listening devices."

"Why do I feel like we've been transported to the set of a James Bond parody movie?" Grace asks dryly.

"We're investigators, not spies," Pedro says with a touch of indignation.

Raphael pipes up, "I thought we were detectives."

Fortunately, Asger changes the subject. "Where did

the whiteboard come from?"

"Sebastien found it for me in a storage room. Isn't it fabulous? We can keep track of our suspects and clues here." Pedro writes Terese at the top of the board in capital letters with a dry erase marker, then proceeds to draw a complicated-looking table underneath. Then he turns and points at Asger and me. "What did you find out from Terese's boyfriend?"

"Ex-boyfriend," I say.

"Once you get to know him, turns out he's a pretty decent guy," Asger says. "Still need to convince him about the merits of country music, but I'm going to work on it."

Pedro frowns. "No, what did you find out from him about the Case of the Missing Violin?"

"He's right. Let's stick to the case." I turn to Pedro and explain that Terese is meeting the buyer at a private party tomorrow night. "According to Nico, the buyer is a man, and he's willing to pay a lot of money for my violin."

While Pedro scrawls a bunch of illegible notes on the whiteboard, J.B. steps forward. "That's where I come in."

"What happened with Terese's roommate?" Asger asks.

J.B. grins. "You mean her ex-roommate."

"What's her name?" Pedro asks.

"Monique." J.B. waits while Pedro jots this down on the whiteboard, then draws a dotted line connecting Monique's name to Terese. Once Pedro signals for him to continue speaking, J.B. fills us in on what Monique told him. "Apparently, Terese showed up early this morning carrying a violin case."

"That would be after she left Nico's," I point out.

"Do you know what time Terese arrived at their apartment?" Pedro asks.

J.B. shrugs. "Not sure. Does it matter?"

"Details are important," Pedro says.

"Why don't you just write down A.M. for now," Sebastien suggests. After Pedro reluctantly agrees, Sebastien nods at J.B. to continue.

"According to Monique, Terese asked if she knew anywhere safe she could store the violin case until tomorrow night. When Monique asked what was wrong with their apartment, Terese said it was the first place they would look. Monique asked who 'they' was, but Terese was cagey."

Grace rolls her eyes. "Yeah, I'd be cagey too if I stole someone's violin."

"Right?" J.B. nods. "Anyway, Terese told Monique that she'd figure something out. She grabbed the violin case and started to leave, but Monique reminded her that she was late with the rent. Terese laughed and said she'd have the money for her after tomorrow night."

"When wasn't Terese late with her rent?" Raphael grumbles. "She was always trying to borrow money from me to pay it."

"You and me both, buddy," J.B. says. "Monique was pretty fed up with it, too. She told Terese to pay up what she owed or find a new place to live. Terese said that was fine with her. She was going to be rolling in money after tomorrow night and wouldn't need to live with a stuck-up cow like her anymore."

I furrow my brow. "Okay, that's all good information. We know Terese had my violin at her apartment this morning and that she's going to sell it at a party tomorrow night, but we still don't know where the party is."

"Ah, but we do.When Terese went into her room to get the rest of her stuff, she left her phone on the kitchen counter. Monique saw a text come through with the details of the party. She didn't think anything of it at the time." J.B. holds up a slip of paper. "Fortunately, Monique has a photographic memory. When I told her what was going on with Jasmine's violin, she jotted down the details."

Pedro grabs the paper from J.B. and waves it in the air triumphantly. "Our first piece of evidence."

After Pedro attaches it to the whiteboard with some silver duct tape, we all rush over to peer at it.

"Does anyone know where that is?" I ask, pointing at the address.

"I do," Sebastien says. "It's a very exclusive private club. Members only."

I cross my fingers. "Please tell me you're a member."

Sebastien puts his arm around my shoulders. "You're in luck. I am."

"Okay, so you can get into the party," Asger points out. "But what about the rest of us?"

"You're not seriously suggesting we all crash the party?" Grace asks.

Asger nods. "You're right. It should just be me and Jasmine."

"That could get tricky," Sebastien says. "Outsiders aren't welcome. I can get the violin myself."

"Be realistic. You're going to need help," Asger says. Then he turns to me. "Besides, I don't think there's any way you could keep Jasmine away."

Sebastien rubs his chin. "You're right. But Terese knows what the two of you look like."

"Disguises," Pedro says enthusiastically. "We can wear disguises."

Asger arches an eyebrow. "We?"

"Yes, the three of us." The Pedro points at the others. "Raphael, Grace, and J.B. will man headquarters while the rest of us carry out the mission."

"But . . ." Asger looks helplessly at me.

"It's easier to give in," I say to Asger.

Asger nods, then says to Pedro, "But no funny costumes, okay?"

CHAPTER 12
FAKE MUSTACHES AND
REALLY BAD WIGS

The next night, Pedro, Asger, and I are standing outside the service entrance to the private club where Terese is supposed to meet the buyer of my violin, waiting for Sebastien to sneak us in.

As a member of the club, Sebastien was able to walk in the front door without pretending to be someone else. In contrast, the three of us are wearing disguises that probably won't stand up to scrutiny. Despite making Pedro swear we wouldn't wear funny costumes on this mission, here we are, looking ridiculous.

Since Asger is supposed to try to pass as one of the guests at the party, he's wearing one of Sebastien's custom-made suits. Although the two men are of similar height, Sebastien has a bit of a paunch, so

Asger has padding underneath his clothes. His white-blond hair is covered by a dark mullet wig, his blue eyes are camouflaged behind large tinted glasses, and he's sporting a fake beard that looked like it was originally used in a Monty Python movie.

My appearance isn't much better. My outfit is supposed to make me look like one of the card dealers working at the club. Most of it is normal–black pencil skirt and vest along with a white button-up shirt. But once you add in the blonde bouffant wig, colored contacts, blue eyeshadow and eyeliner, and a large green dealer's visor that covers my face, I look like a failed Dolly Parton impersonator who ended up having to work at a casino to make ends meet.

Since Terese has never met Pedro, he didn't need to wear a disguise. But there was no way he was going to pass up the opportunity. Asger and I convinced him to pose as a waiter, but, naturally, Pedro had to add his own flair. I have to admit that the port-wine birthmark on his left cheek and scar on his chin look very realistic. But the fake handlebar mustache he's wearing keeps threatening to fall off his face.

Pedro had been the one to source all of our disguises. I'm still not sure how he did it in such a short period of time. To be honest, I'm afraid to ask. If he ever decides to give up playing the viola professionally, he should seriously consider opening up a costume shop.

"Do you think Sebastien forgot about us?" Asger

asks as he paces back and forth by the service entrance.

"He just texted," I remind him. "He's stuck talking to someone. He'll be here as soon as he can."

Pedro pushes the left side of his mustache back into position. "Do you think Terese is wearing a disguise, too?"

"If so, I hope it's different from mine," I say. "The last thing we need are two Dolly Parton look-alikes running around inside there."

Asger chuckles as he shoves his hands in his pockets. "Terese is probably dressed like herself. The point of meeting the buyer at this particular club is that it's private. She's not expecting to run into anyone she knows here."

"But how is she going to hide the fact that she's carrying a violin case?" I ask. "That's not exactly something you bring to a club, is it? Folks are here to drink and gamble, not listen to someone play the violin."

"You're breaking character. Dolly would call it a fiddle," Asger says with a mischievous twinkle in his eye. "Hey, speaking of violins and fiddles, how did the recital go last night? You never said."

"The violin Sebastien borrowed for me sounded terrible," I say. "But the rest of the quartet played brilliantly, as usual."

Pedro shakes his head. "Jasmine is being modest. She was great."

Before I can argue with him, the service entrance door creaks open. Sebastien motions for us to come in. "Hurry up, before someone sees you," he says in hushed tones.

We follow Sebastien down a dimly lit hallway to a storage room. Once we're safely inside, he closes the door, then leans against a metal shelving unit and exhales slowly. "Being a spy is stressful. I was afraid someone was going to ask me what I was doing back here."

"We're detectives, not spies." Pedro pulls an enamel pin out of his pocket and hands it to Sebastien. "See?"

Sebastien smiles as he examines the pin. As he hands it back to Pedro, he asks, "Where did you get this?"

"What is it?" I ask.

"It's a prototype for our official Musical Detectives Agency pin," Pedro explains.

"Wow, you're really taking this seriously," Asger says.

I bite back a smile, then suggest we focus on getting my violin back. "There will be time to look at the pin later . . . assuming we're successful."

Pedro nods. "Okay. The t-shirts won't be here until next week, anyway."

"Don't worry, we'll be successful." Asger squeezes my hand, then turns to Sebastien. "Did you see Terese out there?"

"No. I only got as far as the main bar before a friend stopped me," Sebastien says. "He got a new polo pony he can't stop raving about. He wanted to get my advice about the best place to stable her in Dubai."

"Polo ponies," I say dryly. "The conversations you rich folks have are on such a different level."

Sebastien gives me side-eye. "Hey, you're the girl who wants to snag a guy who is loaded so you can live a champagne and caviar lifestyle."

I gulp. The truth of what Sebastien says hits me hard. Ever since I was a little girl, I've always had my heart set on marrying someone rich. Bonus points if he was a royal. It's not an unusual fantasy–lots of girls wish they could meet a real-life Prince Charming who would sweep them off their feet and away to a luxurious castle.

As I got older, reality set in and I tempered my expectations. Deep down inside I still hoped that I'd meet a billionaire who could give me everything my heart desired, but I knew the odds of it happening were slim.

But after Turd Face swindled me out of my life savings, my dreams of a champagne and caviar-filled life resurfaced big time. A relationship with financial security became paramount. Falling in love, less so.

Then I ran into Asger after all those years apart and now I'm doubting everything. What do I really want out of life? More importantly, *who* do I want in my life?

* * *

"Earth to Jasmine," Asger says, interrupting my ruminations about romantic relationships. "We need to get going."

Is it my imagination or is Asger's manner toward me colder? Geez, of course it is. Sebastien pretty much told everyone how shallow I am. That I have my sights set on nabbing a rich guy, something Asger is not. A waiter and struggling musician hardly fits the bill. Sure, Asger and his band may very well win the Riviera Musical Rodeo competition and land a recording contract, but there's no guarantee they'll make it big.

Let's face it–Asger is probably thinking one of two things right now. One, I'm going to dump him the minute someone richer comes along. Or, two, I'm only with him because I think he is going to be the next global country music sensation and start raking in the money. I'm surprised he doesn't turn and walk out of here, leaving me to get my violin back from Terese by myself.

The cynical side of me whispers in my ear, "He needs you and your violin for the finals this weekend. Without you playing the fiddle, Whiskey and Bragi don't stand a chance. He'll help you get Joshua back, then once his band wins the competition, you're history."

I ball my hands into fists, pressing my fingernails into my palms. The sharp pain keeps me from screaming in frustration at myself. My emotions are so tangled up right now I can't make sense of what's true.

After taking a deep breath, then letting it out slowly, I look in turn at each of the three men standing in this crowded storage room with me. "I'd understand if you guys want to back out. This is my problem, not yours. Based on what I've learned about Terese over these past few days, I worry about how she'll react if she's backed into a corner. And this buyer of hers? How desperate are they to get their hands on my violin? Could their desperation turn violent?"

"I'm with you one hundred percent of the way," Sebastien says.

"Me, too." Pedro looks at the Musical Detectives Agency pin in his hands and grins. "I'm having a blast."

After giving Sebastien and Pedro a grateful smile, I look over at Asger. He's staring at the floor, as though considering his options. "It's okay," I say to him. "I understand. This isn't your fight."

Asger lifts his head and locks his eyes with me. "Don't you get it, Jasmine? I'll always be in your corner. This is our fight."

I blink hard, trying to hold back the tears welling in my eyes. Then I clear my throat. "Okay, what's our game plan?"

"I think we should split up so we can cover more ground," Sebastien suggests. "Jasmine, since you're dressed as a dealer, why don't you take the casino area with Asger?"

"You guys realize I don't actually know how to deal cards, right?" I say. "What if someone asks me to take over? Or worse, what if the other dealers realize I don't belong here?"

"You're in luck. The casino manager isn't here tonight. His wife just had a baby. So if anyone asks, tell them that you're a new hire and learning the ropes." Sebastien turns to Pedro. "With your waiter's disguise, it makes sense for you to stake out the bar. Try to avoid taking any drink orders, if you can."

"What about you?" I ask Sebastien.

"I'll be a roamer," he replies. "The casino and bar are the two main areas of the club, but there are also the bathrooms, main entrance, and the back rooms to keep an eye on. Everyone keep their cell phones on. If you spot Terese, text the rest of the group. Just remember to keep your cool, and don't scare her off."

"I wish we could use walkie-talkies instead of our cell phones," Pedro says wistfully. "Like the Three Investigators did."

"Who are the Three Investigators?" Asger asks.

"It's an old series of detective books for kids," I explain.

Sebastien pats Pedro on the back. "Maybe we can get walkie-talkies for our next investigation. But today, we're going to stick with our phones."

When Pedro's eyes light up at the mention of the possibility of a future investigation, I smile. Pedro might be thinking about a career change after all this. Being a professional musician will seem positively boring after getting a taste of sneaking around undercover.

"Okay, we should get going," Sebastien says.

After a group handshake, Pedro adjusts his fake mustache, Asger checks to make sure his mullet wig isn't askew, and I pull my green dealer's visor down over my eyes. Yeah, no one is going to see through these amateur disguises of ours.

Sebastien pokes his head out of the storage room to check that the coast is clear. Then we all hustle to our assigned positions.

As Asger and I enter the casino, my jaw drops. It's like we've been transported into the interior of a crystal ice cave. Everything is made out of sleek, blue-white reflective materials which look like they would be cold to the touch. Realistic-looking stalagmites hang from the ceiling, ice sculptures are dotted around the room, and a mist swirls around our feet, obscuring the floor. The only pops of color come from the gaming tables and the evening dresses the ladies are wearing.

"This is wild," I say in hushed tones to Asger.

"Wild is one word for it," he says. "But I guess this is how the rich and famous roll."

I chew on my bottom lip, desperately wanting to clear the air after Sebastien's comment about me wanting to snag someone with money. But now is not the time. Instead, I ask, "Do you see Terese anywhere?"

Asger scans the room. "No, but there's a lot of people here. Come on, let's walk around."

When I instinctively grab for his hand, he gives me a funny look. I quickly release it when he says, "You're blowing our cover. We're not a couple . . . at least not here." The way he says it sounds more like a question than a statement.

I mentally shake myself. Concentrate on finding Terese and Joshua right now. Deal with your feelings later.

We walk through the casino, taking pains not to make it seem like we're together. No one seems to notice either of us—everyone is too wrapped up in gambling away obscene amounts of money. Even the casino employees don't pay any attention, their focus solely on taking bets, dealing cards, and spinning roulette wheels.

Someone brushes past me, nearly knocking me into one of the ice sculptures. As I regain my balance,

I stare at the woman's retreating back. There's something off about her figure-hugging fuchsia dress. It takes me a moment to realize what it is, then it hits me. It's clearly an off-the-rack dress, not a designer one made out of exquisite material and custom tailored to fit the wearer. No one in this casino would be wearing something so ordinary, so middle-class, unless they didn't belong here. And the only people who don't belong here are Pedro, Sebastien, Asger and . . . Terese.

My eyes travel up to the woman's head. Just as I thought–dark hair worn in loose curls. I don't need to see her face to know that she's wearing heavy makeup. It's Terese without a doubt. But where's my violin? The only thing Terese is carrying is an evening bag.

I try to get Asger's attention, but he's facing the other direction. Grabbing my phone out of my pocket, I quickly type a group text while following after Terese at a discreet distance.

Quarry spotted in casino. In pursuit. No sight of Joshua.

After pressing send, I look back up, but Terese is gone. I push forward through the crowd, trying desperately to spot her. A man grabs my elbow and I yank it away. "Hey, honey, want to be my Lady Luck?" he calls out after me, slurring his words. Cheers erupt from a craps table as I near it, someone clearly thrilled to have won big. I dart around the people having a celebratory embrace, then I'm stopped in my tracks by one of the real dealers.

"Oh, good. You're here." She points at a poker table where three gentlemen are seated. "Watch out for the guy on the right. There's something fishy about him."

"Um, no, you don't understand. I'm new," I splutter. "I can't deal cards."

"It's okay, we all have to start somewhere," she says cheerfully to me. "Besides, it's time for my break."

I wait until she walks away, then quickly resume my search for Terese, leaving the poker players wondering what happened to their dealer.

As I'm searching behind one of the stalagmites, Asger comes up behind me. "Is your phone on silent? You haven't been answering our texts."

"Oh, crap. Sorry. Do you know where she is?" I ask, my voice squeaky with anxiety. "I lost her."

"Pedro said she's in the bar. Come on." Asger grabs my hand, apparently now unconcerned that we might appear to be a couple.

We rush into the main hallway and I spot a flash of fuchsia out of the corner of my eye. "I think that's her," I whisper. "I think Terese just went into that room."

"What room?" Asger asks.

Instead of answering, I sprint down the hallway. When I reach the room Terese entered seconds ago, I yank the door open, prepared to confront my nemesis. Instead, all I see is one of the car valets sitting on a folding chair looking at his phone. The room is bare except for a broom and dustpan in the corner, a file cabinet and coat rack on one wall, and a board with keys hanging from it on the opposite wall.

"Where did she go?" I mutter.

The valet glances at me. "Huh?"

I hear Asger behind me, asking the valet more forcefully where the woman with dark hair is.

"She's wearing a fuchsia dress," I add.

"That way," the valet says, pointing behind him. That's when I realize there are two entrances to this room we're in–the one Asger and I just came in and another next to the coat rack, presumably leading outside.

Asger moves quickly, pushing open the other door. I'm right behind him, screaming Terese's name at the top of my lungs. There's a black sports car at the end of the gravel drive, its engine running. I spot a man putting something in the trunk, then slam it shut. He has his back toward me, so I can't see what he's put in the trunk. But my gut is telling me that it's Joshua.

For some reason, I'm frozen in place, unable to move. I watch as Asger grabs the man by the shoulders, but the other man overpowers him, pushing Asger to the ground. Asger tries to get back up, but the other man is too quick, kicking Asger in the gut. Seeing Asger writhe in pain is what finally jolts me into action.

As I rush over to help Asger, the other man opens up the driver's side of the car. But before he slips inside, I catch a glimpse of his face and gasp. It's none other than Prince Oboroten.

CHAPTER 13
A CAT BURGLAR TO THE RESCUE

"You really should have a doctor check you out," Grace says to Asger as she applies antibacterial ointment to the scrapes on his face.

Asger is sitting on the couch in the music room at Sebastien's villa or, as Pedro insists on calling it, the Musical Detectives Agency Headquarters. After our run-in with Prince Oboroten at the private club, Sebastien and Pedro tried unsuccessfully to chase after the prince's car while I tended to Asger.

The poor guy was banged up pretty badly–bruising on his abdomen from where the prince had kicked him, cuts on his face from smacking into the gravel driveway, and a sprained ankle from being forcibly thrown to the ground. Grace was right. Asger should have gone directly to the ER to ensure there weren't any other injuries, but he stubbornly refused, saying it would be a waste of time.

When I had suggested calling the police to file a report about how the prince assaulted Asger and stole my violin, Sebastien counseled against it. "Obie has friends in high places. Any report you file will probably 'disappear,'" he said ominously. "We have to outsmart him. I'm just not sure how to do that yet."

After arguing with Asger for a few minutes about going to the hospital, Sebastien, Pedro, and I gave up. The guys had helped him up and into Sebastien's car. Then we all headed back to HQ, where we are now, to meet back up with J.B., Raphael, and Grace.

"Ouch." Asger grimaces, then grabs the antibacterial ointment and bandages from Grace. "Let me do it." But as he gets to his feet, he groans with pain when he puts his weight on his bad ankle.

I rush over and help him settle back on the couch. "Let Grace take care of you. You're in no condition to be walking around."

"Some knight in shining armor I turned out to be," Asger mutters as I plump up a cushion behind his back.

"Are you kidding me?" I perch on an ottoman next to the couch. "You tried to stop the prince."

Asger shakes his head. "But I got beaten up, and he got away. Doesn't really fit the job description."

"You were brave," I point out. "That's what a knight in shining armor is. Someone who is willing to put themselves in harm's way to help someone else.

In fact, I think you deserve a promotion from knight to king of shining armor."

"Here, here," Sebastien says.

Pedro hands Asger the Musical Detective Agency pin. "You should wear this in recognition of your selfless act of bravery."

"For those of us who weren't there, can you fill us in on exactly what happened at the club?" Raphael asks.

"Wait a minute." Pedro wheels the whiteboard over closer to Asger, then motions for everyone to take a seat.

Pedro is stumped for a minute, not wanting to write over the complicated table and diagrams he had drawn on the whiteboard earlier in the evening. When Grace suggests using the other side, Pedro nearly knocks Asger in the head as he swivels the whiteboard around.

"Whoa, watch the noggin," Asger says to Pedro.

"Sorry," Pedro mumbles. He tries turning the whiteboard in the other direction only to end up bumping into the coffee table, causing a can of soda to flip into the air and land on Raphael's lap.

As Raphael rushes into the bathroom to clean the spilt soda off his pants, the Persian cat makes an appearance. Apparently, according to feline logic, now is the perfect time to try to untie the laces on J.B.'s shoes. When the cat is firmly told that shoelaces aren't toys, he hacks up a hairball on the carpet.

While all this is happening, Pedro has discovered that one of the dry erase markers is leaking and now he has black ink all over his hands. When his fake mustache threatens to fall off his face for the millionth time tonight, Pedro presses it back in place, transferring some of the ink to his face.

It's starting to feel like one of those old *Three Stooges* episodes. The fact that Asger, Pedro, and I are still wearing our ridiculous costumes doesn't help either. Although, I guess it was a blessing that Asger was sporting a fake beard, as it had protected the majority of his face from gravel scrapes.

Grace helps Pedro get the ink off his hands and face and J.B. and Raphael reposition the whiteboard while I clean up the cat's hairball. Then I yank my dealer's visor and Dolly Parton wig off my head and fluff up my hair. Asger rubs his chin tentatively, takes a deep breath, then pulls the fake beard off his face, yelping as the adhesive tears at his skin.

Once order is restored, and we all look more or less normal again, Pedro gets everyone's attention. Using a functioning dry erase marker, he scrawls 'Field Report' at the top of the whiteboard, then motions to me to give an update on what transpired at the club.

"It's a pretty simple update," I say. "After spotting Terese in the casino, Asger and I followed her out into the hallway. Then she disappeared into a room which turned out to be where the valets store car keys and hang out during their breaks. Unfortunately, Terese slipped out the door that leads outside before we could catch up with her. We ran out after her and that's when we saw Prince Oboroten putting something in the trunk of his car."

Raphael leans forward. "Was it your violin?"

"I didn't get a close look at it," I say. "But it has to have been Joshua."

"The valet confirmed that Terese had left the violin in that room before she went into the casino to meet the prince," Asger says. "She slipped him a wad of cash to keep an eye on it."

"That's right. After she made contact with Prince Oboroten, she went back to retrieve the violin." I readjust my position on the ottoman, then explain how I lost sight of Terese while I was following her in the casino. "That's when she must have connected with the prince. He told her to meet him outside with the violin."

"We know the prince took off in his car, but how did Terese get away?" J.B. asks.

"Oh, she was with him," I say. "Right before he sped off, Terese rolled down the passenger window and gave us the finger."

J.B. shakes his head. "Classy."

"How did Terese hook up with the prince in the first place?" Raphael asks. "Did they know each other before?"

"I think they might have met at the prince's birthday party," J.B. says. "Terese and I were both there working as catering staff. I saw her chatting with the prince that night. When I went over to tell her that she was needed in the kitchen, I overheard her say something to the prince about koalas and kangaroos. Despite the fact I knew Jasmine's violin has those same animals engraved on it, at the time, I didn't put two and two together."

"They were talking about the distinctive engravings on my Avestruz violin." I pause for a moment while Pedro sketches a violin with a koala and kangaroo on the whiteboard. It's a remarkably good likeness. Continuing, I say, "The prince had already expressed an interest in buying Joshua from me, which I refused to do. When our quartet performed at his party, seeing me play my violin again might have made him want it even more. Then when Terese told him she could get it for him, well . . . we all know what happened next."

Grace looks thoughtful as she strokes the cat, who is now sleeping in her lap. "So, if we can't go to the police, how are we going to get Jasmine's violin back?"

"We have to figure out where the violin is in the first place," Raphael points out.

"Oh, I know exactly where it is," I say. "When I was at the prince's villa previously, he showed me the gallery where he keeps all his treasures. He already had a spot picked out for my violin in his gallery, right next to an antique harpsichord."

"Knowing where it is makes it easier." J.B. rubs his hands together. "Now, all we have to do is sneak in and get it back."

Pedro grins. "Can we wear disguises?"

"No more disguises," I say firmly. "They wouldn't help, anyway. There's no way we're going to be able to break into the prince's house, let alone the gallery. The place is like Fort Knox. We'd never be able to get past the alarm system, let alone the retina scanner."

Everyone is silent after that. I start to imagine what my life will be like without Joshua. The odds of getting him back are faint. As my eyes start to water, Sebastien clears his throat.

"There may be a way we can get into the prince's villa and gallery," he says. "I have to warn you, though, it's a long shot."

I press my hands together in a pleading gesture. "Whatever it is, we have to try."

Sebastien gets to his feet. "Okay, let me go make a call and see what I can do."

"Who are you going to call?" Asger asks.

"An old family friend," Sebastien says slowly. "Who just happens to be a former jewel thief."

* * *

The next evening, the gang regroups at HQ to meet Sebastien's old family friend. As we wait in the music room, I think back to the last time Sebastien brought a guest to meet the members of the quartet–namely, Prince Oboroten. That was when the prince first set eyes on my Avestruz, coveting it immediately. At first he had offered to buy it, but when I refused, he resorted to having Terese steal it for him.

As Grace serves us coffee and Pedro passes around a tray of macaroons, Sebastien ushers in a man who looks to be in his late sixties or early seventies. His hair and beard are white, although based on his coloring and the touch of russet in his facial hair, I suspect he was a redhead when he was younger. The tweed jacket, blue button-down shirt, and khaki pants he's wearing give him a professorial air, and the expression on his face is jovial.

"Everyone, allow me to present Hamish MacDougall," Sebastien says.

"So this is the Musical Detectives Agency I've heard so much about," Hamish says with an accent that brings bagpipes, kilts, and *Outlander* to mind.

Grace must be thinking the same thing because she asks Hamish if he's from Scotland.

"Aye, lassie," the older man says. "And where might you be from? You have a lovely, soft accent."

"Canada." She smiles as she taps her chest. "I'm Grace, the other violinist in the Fjura Quartet."

The others introduce themselves in turn. When Pedro says that he's from the Mexican state of Oaxaca, Hamish's eyes light up. "I have a holiday planned there. I can't wait to see the archaeological sites, especially Monte Albán."

"Let me know when you'll be there. My family can show you around," Pedro offers. "I'll also be home visiting in a few months. Maybe our trips will overlap."

After the two men have a brief chat about the must-see attractions in Oaxaca, Hamish turns to me. "And you must be Jasmine, the poor lassie who had her violin stolen."

I chew on my bottom lip. "Do you really think you can get Joshua back?"

"Joshua? Is that the name of your violin?" Hamish cocks his head to one side. I nod, then Hamish asks, "Did you name him after Joshua Bell by any chance?"

My jaw drops. "How did you know that?"

"You're a violinist. Joshua Bell is a violinist." Hamish spreads his hands out as though it's crystal clear. "Makes perfect sense."

"He's the greatest violinist of our time," I say reverently.

"Aye, lassie, but I bet you give him a run for his money." Hamish smiles at me, then turns to the group. "Well, shall we get started? From what Sebastien told me, Jasmine needs her violin back as quick as can be."

J.B. furrows his brow. "We have the finals for the Riviera Musical Rodeo on Saturday night. That's in three days' time. We're essentially talking about planning and executing a heist from a place with some serious security measures. How are we going to pull that off?"

"We also need time to rehearse," Raphael points out.

"No need to worry, lads," Hamish says. "I have experience with this sort of thing."

Asger leans forward. "Sebastien says you're a jewel thief."

"I prefer the term 'cat burglar,'" Hamish says. "Has a more elegant ring to it, don't you think? And just for the record, I'm an *ex*-cat burglar."

Grace arches an eyebrow. "Sounds like there's a story there."

"There is indeed. But it's best told over a wee dram or two of single malt whisky, and we don't have time for that now," Hamish says. "Our target will be on the move tomorrow night, and that's when we'll strike."

Sebastien nods. "That's right. Remember that friend of mine I ran into at the club? The one who got a new polo pony? Well, he told me that Obie is going to fly him to Dubai tomorrow on his private jet and show him where he stables his ponies."

Pedro looks up from the whiteboard where he's been scribbling notes. "So the coast will be clear."

"Hang on a minute," J.B. says. "The prince will be gone, but what about his staff?"

"I have a plan for that." Sebastien rubs his hands together. "Remember that guy that stood Jasmine up at the casino?"

"Wow, that seems like a lifetime ago," I say. "How is he involved in this?"

"I'll get to that," Sebastien says. "Let me tell you my idea first. Our housekeeper and gardener are coming back tomorrow morning from their month-long honeymoon. My parents have booked them into a suite at the Hotel Metropole for a couple of nights before they start back at work."

Sebastien takes a sip of his coffee, then tells us that the prince's staff and his family's housekeeper and gardener are all good friends. "I'm going to arrange a little welcome home dinner for the newlyweds so they can celebrate with their friends. It's the perfect excuse to ensure the prince's staff are away from the villa tomorrow night."

"I'm still now sure how Mr. No Show fits into this," I say.

"The party is going to take place in a private dining room at an exclusive seafood restaurant. I'll make sure the champagne flows all evening." Sebastien grins. "The owner happens to be a good friend of mine, and he also happens to have good reason to despise Mr. No Show. So when it comes time to pay the bill, he's going to charge it to Mr. No Show's account."

I furrow my brow. "But won't Mr. No Show refuse to pay it?"

"Not when he finds out that the guests included the prince's staff," Sebastien says. "He'll think footing the bill will ingratiate himself with Obie."

"It sounds perfect," I say. "Your housekeeper and gardener have a nice time with their friends, and Mr. No Show pays for it."

"Okay, that takes care of getting the prince's staff out of the villa tomorrow night," J.B. says. "But how do we get inside the place?"

"Do you mind getting things set up?" Sebastien asks Pedro. "Hamish emailed you the file."

Pedro is in his element. He hooks up his laptop to a projector, then pulls down a portable screen. When he powers up the laptop, the Musical Detectives Agency logo appears on the screen. "Wait a minute," Pedro says. "I forgot to turn on the sound."

Music starts playing. It's full of bright notes, a catchy rhythm, and has a peppy ending. When it finishes, Pedro surveys the room. "What do you think?"

"It sounds familiar, like a television theme song," Raphael says.

"It's *our* theme song." Pedro grins. "I composed it yesterday."

Grace groans. "We're just trying to get Jasmine's violin back, not become a TV and movie franchise."

"Maybe you should pull up the file," Sebastien suggests gently.

"Okay." Pedro shrugs and presses a few buttons on his laptop.

Hamish walks over to the screen and motions for

Pedro to click through the slides. "This is the floor plan for the prince's villa and schematics for his security system."

"How did you get a hold of these?" Asger asks.

"That's probably a question better left unanswered." Hamish spits out a bunch of gobbledygook about alarms, codes, and sensors, then smiles at us. "As you can see, it will be a piece of cake."

The rest of us exchange looks. If Hamish's idea of a 'piece of cake' is an impregnable system designed to keep intruders out, then sure, this is that. But that's not generally how I define a 'piece of cake.' When I say as much, Sebastien reassures me that Hamish will be able to get us into the prince's villa.

"Okay, assuming that's the case," I say, "we still have to get into the gallery. How are we going to get past the retina scanner without the prince's . . . um . . . retina?"

Grace blanches. "Please tell me we're not going to–"

"No, lassie, that's not how I operate," Hamish says firmly. "Let's just say I have contacts with a certain international spy agency who has graciously provided me with the necessary technology to get past the retina scanner."

"Phew." Grace visibly relaxes. Then she gives Hamish a curious look. "Why do I feel like you have a lot of stories to tell?"

"Och, aye. But most of them I can't tell." Hamish

winks at Grace, then turns back to the group. "Now, we need to keep the team small. Just Jasmine, me, and a getaway driver."

"Getaway driver, that's me." Asger leaps to his feet, then winces.

"You're in no condition to drive a car," I tell Asger. "You need to rest that sprained ankle of yours."

Pedro waves his hands in the air. "Pick me! Pick me!"

Hamish looks at him dubiously. "Have you ever driven a getaway car?"

"Do go-carts count?" Pedro asks.

"Not quite." Hamish glances at the rest of us. "Anyone else have experience with this sort of thing?"

J.B. chuckles. "In driving a getaway car? In case you haven't noticed, we're musicians. I'm pretty sure I can speak for the rest of us in saying this is our first heist. Getaway cars, cracking security systems, stealing violins–"

"It's not stealing," I say. "Joshua belongs to me."

"I stand corrected," J.B. says. "Restoring violins to their rightful owners and getting past retina scanners isn't exactly in our wheelhouse."

"I got a speeding ticket once," Pedro says as proof of his getaway car driver credentials. "The police officer said I was driving really fast."

I bite back a smile, then say to Hamish, "It's easier to give in, trust me."

Hamish pats Pedro on the back. "Okay, you're in."

As Pedro lets out a whoop and does a fist pump, I shake my head. "But there's one condition."

"What's that?" Pedro asks.

I narrow my eyes. "No funny costumes, okay?"

CHAPTER 14
WHY IS IT ALWAYS LASERS?

It feels like déjà vu. Twenty-four hours have elapsed since everyone was last assembled in the music room at Sebastien's villa. Everyone is sipping coffee and munching on macaroons while they talk about getting back my violin from Prince Oboroten. There is one big difference, though. The discussion yesterday was about hypotheticals, tossing around options for breaking into the prince's villa. Today it's about actually doing it.

No wonder I feel sick to my stomach. Hamish, Pedro, and I are going to try to pull off a heist that would give the guys from Ocean's Eleven a run for their money. I dread to think about what will happen if we get caught.

There's another reason I feel like I'm going to throw up. Even if we get my violin back, I'm not sure

Whiskey and Bragi will be able to compete in the Riviera Music Rodeo finals. During the semi-finals, the prince might not have figured out that I was playing the fiddle instead of Terese, but he sure as heck knows about our subterfuge now. The question is, will he eliminate Whiskey and Bragi for breaking the competition rules? And if he doesn't, won't he notice that I'm playing the very same violin he stole from me and which is now missing from his gallery?

When I mentioned my concerns earlier to Asger, he told me not to worry about it. "Let's cross that bridge when we get to it," he had said. Then he kissed me and my fears momentarily faded into the background. They're back in full force now, though.

"You sure you don't want a macaroon?" Grace asks me. "You barely ate anything at dinner."

I shake my head. "Too many nerves."

Grace sits next to me and squeezes my hand. "You can always back out. There has to be another way to get Joshua."

"You heard what Sebastien said yesterday." I chew on my bottom lip. "The prince has a lot of connections. Even if the police believe me, they won't want to risk crossing him just to get my violin back."

"I guess you're right." Grace glances over at Hamish. "I really want to hear that man's backstory. Imagine meeting a real life cat burglar."

"Ex-cat burglar," I remind her. "He seems to be on the straight and narrow."

"I'm not so sure about that," Grace says. "Instead of stealing jewelry for his own profit, I think he's more like Robin Hood now."

"Stealing from the rich to give to the poor?" I chuckle. "Considering the state of my bank account, I guess I qualify as the poor."

Pedro whistles to get everyone's attention. He's standing next to the projection screen. But instead of the floor plans and security schematics that were displayed on it yesterday, today there's a countdown clock ticking down the minutes until we need to depart for the prince's villa.

"Sebastien has confirmed that the prince's staff has left for the party," Pedro says. "The mission team will leave here in thirty minutes. We'll wait outside the villa until we get word that the prince's private plane has taken off for Dubai. It's scheduled to depart one hour from now. Are there any final questions?"

Everyone seems clear on their roles and the plan: Hamish and I are the team on the ground, Pedro is driving the getaway car, Sebastien and Asger are manning the communications center, Grace is in charge of refreshments, and J.B. and Raphael are on standby in case anything goes wrong.

I start laughing hysterically as I think about everything that could go wrong.

Asger's brow is creased with worry. "Are you okay, Jasmine?"

"I'm fine," I say after doing a few deep breathing

exercises. My phone buzzes, startling me. "I have to take this. It's my friend Olivia."

"Hey, there. This is a surprise," I say as I walk into the kitchen. "I thought you were swamped with the construction project on that Greek island."

"Let's do video chat," Olivia suggests. "I have someone who wants to say hi."

"Sure." I grab a bottle of sparkling water from the fridge, then prop my phone up on the kitchen island. When Olivia's aunt appears on the screen, I squeal with delight. "Celeste, it's been ages."

"It's been far too long, dear," she says with a smile.

Celeste looks polished and put together, as always. Her hair and makeup are stylish, but she doesn't try to hide her age. Growing old gracefully is something I admire. She must be in her late sixties now, possibly even seventy, but she has the energy of someone half her age.

"Something told me that you and I need to have a chat," Celeste says. "You're in danger, aren't you?"

My eyes widen. "Danger? Um, why would you say that?" I splutter, wondering how she could know about the break-in we have planned.

"Your heart, dear," Celeste gives me a gentle smile. "You're in danger of losing your heart and falling in love."

Olivia pops her head on screen and grins. "Aunt Celeste has been consulting her crystals again. Don't worry, you're not the only person whose love life she meddles in."

Celeste shoos Olivia away, then turns back to me. "So, is it true or not?"

I feel butterflies fluttering in my stomach, but I'm not sure if they're related to the anxiety I'm feeling about our heist. My pulse races as I think about Celeste's question–am I falling in love with Asger? I take a sip of my water, stalling for time before answering her.

I hear someone clearing their throat behind me. Spinning around on my stool, I see Hamish standing in the doorway. He points at his watch, mouthing, "We need to get going." Then he looks at my water and gives me a questioning look. I motion at the fridge, and he walks over there and pulls out a bottle while I turn back to my phone.

"Celeste, I'm sorry. I actually can't chat now. The, um . . ." My voice trails off as I figure out what to say. I can't exactly tell her that there's a former cat burglar standing in the kitchen waiting for me so we can break into a prince's villa. So, I go with a variation of the truth. "Um, the locksmith is here. I need him to help me get into something."

"Did you lock your keys in your car?" Celeste asks. "I had that happen to me once."

"Jasmine doesn't drive anymore," Olivia says off camera.

"It's something like that," I say quickly. "Anyway, let's chat later, okay?"

After I end the video, Hamish gives me a thoughtful look. "That woman you were talking to. How do you know her?"

"Why don't I explain on the way?" I grab my bottle of water, then turn back to Hamish. "Thanks again for doing this. I'll find a way to repay you somehow."

"Don't be silly, lassie," he says. "I haven't had this much fun in ages."

* * *

Sebastien walks Hamish, Pedro, and I down to the garage. As he's handing Pedro the keys to the Range Rover, a voice calls out behind us. "Wait for me."

I shake my head as Asger limps toward us. "Pedro has this. You should be upstairs with Sebastien manning the communications center."

"First of all, our communications center consists of our cell phones. It's not a bunch of high-tech equipment in a secure, climate-controlled room," Asger points out. "Second, cell phones are portable, meaning I can take mine with me wherever I go. And I'm going with you."

"You can't operate a vehicle with that ankle of yours," I say.

Hamish frowns. "I appreciate your determination, laddie, but you need to sit this one out."

"Exactly." Asger opens the front passenger door. "I'm going to *sit* in the car. I know I can't be part of the action, but I can be there to support the woman I . . ."

As his voice trails off, I draw my breath in sharply. "The woman you what?"

Asger gives me a sheepish grin. "Later, okay?"

I nod in agreement, then we all get into the vehicle. Once Pedro starts the car, Sebastien taps the roof, then waves goodbye as we pull out of the garage. Pedro drives smoothly through the streets of Monte Carlo, easing some of my concerns about having him as our getaway driver.

Some, not all. When push comes to shove, I'm not sure how he'll hold up under pressure. I'm not sure how I'll hold up either.

When we reach the prince's villa, Pedro pulls into a spot at the end of the block. I stare out the window while we wait for Sebastien to call with the all-clear. The guys make small talk about soccer, or football, as they call it. I think about what it will be like to have Joshua back in my possession.

When Asger's phone rings, I nearly jump out of my skin. Then I smile, realizing that his ringtone is *9 to 5* by Dolly Parton. *What would Dolly do in a situation like this?* I ask myself. She'd attack it with grace and confidence, and a healthy dose of humor.

As I channel my inner Dolly, Asger lets us know that the prince's plane has taken off. "He's on his way to Dubai. It's time to put Operation Joshua into action."

After Hamish and I get out of the car, I smooth down my pullover top. It's black, like my joggers, tennies, and baseball cap. Hamish is dressed similarly. I stifle a laugh as I realize I'm now wearing the unofficial uniform of cat burglars–dark to blend into the shadows and with shoes you can sprint away in if you're caught.

I send up a silent prayer, then follow Hamish up the road to the prince's villa. There's an imposing metal gate at the entrance. It's solid, so I can't see through to the other side, which is a bit disconcerting. Although Sebastien has told me repeatedly that the prince doesn't have guard dogs, I worry that we'll be greeted by a vicious Doberman or German Shepherd intent on protecting its master's property.

As I press my ear to the gate, listening for sounds of canines on the prowl, Hamish pulls out a small electronic device out of the zippered pocket of his belt bag. He attaches it to a keypad on one of the gate pillars. There's a slight humming noise, then the gate silently glides open.

Hamish snatches his device off the keypad, then grabs my arm. "Come on, lassie."

Thankfully, the only creature we're greeted by is a peacock strutting through the lush gardens in front of the prince's villa. I don't remember him from the last time I was here. Perhaps the prince won him in a poker game, like he did with the swans.

I gulp as the gate closes behind us. There's no turning back now. Hamish is already at the front door, his electronic device working its magic. Quickly darting to catch up with him, I stumble, landing on the circular gravel driveway. It reminds me of Asger's bravery confronting the prince at the club. Thinking about that gives me the focus I need.

I get back to my feet and rush inside. The main hallway has been completely transformed. Instead of the excessive gilding and mirrored surfaces that previously adorned it, now the space has a jungle feel. Dark green walls, tropical birds in cages suspended from the ceiling, ferns and flowering plants crammed in every corner, and leopard print carpeting on the floor.

Hamish is standing in front of a marble staircase stroking his beard. "Are you sure we haven't stepped into a theme park, lassie?"

"No, this is the prince's villa," I say. "Apparently, he's in his leopard era."

Hamish shakes his head, then tells me to lead the way. As we climb the stairs, I look around for the cameras that we had seen on the schematics. Despite Hamish assuring us that they've been deactivated, I'm still worried we'll be caught on tape.

When we get to the top of the stairs, I point in the direction of the gallery. I trail after Hamish, the combination of the thick carpet and my tennis shoes masking the sounds of our footfalls. Sweat beads on my forehead when we reach the entrance to the gallery. We may have made it this far without a hitch, but the retina scanner is the real test.

As Hamish pulls a small plastic case out of his belt bag, I wonder what else he has in there besides devices designed to bypass security systems. A granola bar, perhaps? My stomach clenches, reminding me that thinking about food isn't helpful right now.

Hamish opens the case, extracts a contact lens, and places it in his right eye. "Moment of truth, lassie." He winks at me, then presses his face up to the scanner. I hold my breath, like I do in tunnels, wishing hard for the fake retina to work.

After what seems like an eternity, a green light flashes from the panel and the door slowly opens. My knees turn to jelly. All I need to do is step inside, and I'll be reunited with my beloved violin. So why am I frozen in place? I thought humans were supposed to have a fight-or-flight reaction in moments of stress. I'm not rushing forward into the gallery and I'm not tearing back down the stairs and fleeing out of the villa. Nope, I'm stuck here in one spot in freeze mode.

If it wasn't for Hamish urging me to get a move on, I think I might have stood there for hours. But his Scottish accent cuts through the fog in my brain, and I slowly put one foot in front of the other. Once I'm inside the gallery, I'm able to move more naturally.

Hamish audibly gasps as we pass one treasure after

another. "I've seen that painting before," he says.

"In the Louvre, right? That one is a copy."

He nods, then points at a sarcophagus. "This was stolen from the Egyptian Museum in Cairo two years ago." After identifying several other priceless items and muttering to himself about how Interpol would be very interested in seeing what the prince has hidden away in his gallery, we arrive at the section containing the prince's prized musical instruments.

When I see Joshua perched on a velvet pillow on top of a marble pedestal, I press my hands to my mouth. Tears roll down my cheeks as I stare at my beloved violin.

Hamish gives me a moment, then places his hand on my shoulder. "Would you like to do the honors, lassie?"

I nod, then walk toward the marble pedestal. As I'm about to reach out and grab Joshua off the velvet pillow, Hamish yells at me to stop.

"Step back slowly." His voice sounds strained. Once I'm a few feet away from my violin, Hamish mutters to himself, "How could I have missed that?"

"Missed what?" I ask, my voice squeaking.

Hamish sighs. "Lasers. Why does it always have to be lasers?"

Tilting my head, I look back at Joshua. That's when I notice the faint blue shimmer surrounding him. "How are we going to get past that?"

Instead of answering me, Hamish unzips his fleece

vest, reaches into the inside pocket and pulls out something that looks like a cross between Harry Potter's wand and one of those laser pointers you used to play with cats. He aims it at the marble pedestal, then waves it around in a figure eight motion.

"Abracadabra," he says before putting the device back in his pocket.

My eyebrows shoot up. "Did you just use a magic spell?"

Hamish chuckles. "No, that was just for comical effect. You look so tense, lassie. Relax. The lasers have been deactivated. You can fetch your violin now."

The thought of lasers searing through my skin is daunting. It takes a bit of persuading on Hamish's part before I dare to approach my violin again. Once I'm standing next to the marble pedestal, I take a deep breath, then grab Joshua and press him to my chest.

"Do you see his case anywhere?" I ask Hamish.

He looks around for a few moments, but comes up empty-handed. "You can always get another case. We'd best be off."

After we slip out of the gallery, the door closes behind us, locking away all the prince's treasures. Sure, some of them he acquired legally, either through purchase or by winning them in a bet, but so many of the items on display inside are stolen. Unfortunately, the chance of them being reunited with their rightful owners is remote. It makes me feel doubly blessed to have my violin back.

As Hamish and I walk back down the marble staircase to the main hallway, the tropical birds start chirping. Their noise is so loud that I almost miss the sound of my phone ringing. Tucking Joshua under one arm, I pause on the bottom step and check to see who's calling.

"It's Asger," I tell Hamish as I put my phone on speaker mode. "We have–"

Before I can finish telling Asger that we have my violin, he interrupts. "Abort! Abort! The prince just pulled up in front of the house."

Hamish locks his eyes with mine. "Listen to me carefully, lassie. You and Joshua are going to go out through the underground garage. Walk up the ramp. The garage door will automatically open when it senses you. Then run as fast as you can to the getaway car. Do you understand?"

"What are you going to do?" I ask in a shaky voice.

"Don't worry about me," he says firmly.

"But–"

Hamish pushes me toward the door that leads to the back stairs. "Go. Now."

I rush downstairs and into the underground garage. The overhead lights are off and the only illumination comes from strip lighting running around the perimeter of the room. I'm disoriented, trying to recall which way the ramp leading out of the garage is. I startle when my phone rings again.

"Where are you?" Asger asks as I press it to my ear.

"In the garage," I say in hushed tones. "Tell Pedro to start the car. I'll be there in a minute."

"Slight problem," Asger says. "Pedro got out of the car to pick some flowers, dropped the keys and they fell into a storm drain."

"Please tell me you're joking."

"I wish I was. We need another vehicle . . . wait a minute, did you say you're in the garage?"

"Yes, but–"

"I know, I know. You haven't driven in a while, but there isn't another choice," he says simply.

I look around at all the vehicles surrounding me, then my eyes land on the blue Citröen deux chevaux the prince tried to gift to me the last time I was here. Peering inside the tiny car, I give a silent cheer when I see the keys hanging in the ignition. Then I groan when I see the gear shift box. Of course, it's a manual drive. This should go well.

"What do you think, Joshua? Can I do it?"

Always the strong, silent type, Joshua doesn't respond. I'm tempted to call Asger and have him tell Pedro to meet me in the garage so he can drive the car when I hear someone coming down the stairs. Based on the heavy tread, I'm pretty sure it isn't Hamish. Cat burglars have a stealthy way of walking.

The prince is going to be here in a matter of

seconds. Time to channel my inner Dolly and drive on out of here.

CHAPTER 15
NO MATTER WHAT THE COST

As I yank the car door open, I listen to the footfall on the metal staircase leading down to the garage. My hands shake as I gently place my violin on the passenger seat. Expecting the prince to burst into the cavernous room any second now, I slip inside the tiny blue car. But the footsteps abruptly stop.

"Please, let him go back upstairs," I whisper to myself. Then my heart sinks as I wonder what happened to Hamish. Why had he been so insistent that I go on without him? Did he try to confront the prince? If so, what happened? Is he okay?

While these fears race through my head, I hear the prince speaking. Because he's still in the stairwell, I can't make out what he's saying. But the tone of his voice tells me that he's angry. Based on the occasional pauses without anyone else responding, I'm guessing he's on his phone. That's good–only one scary person chasing after me.

I quickly familiarize myself with the car while the prince is distracted by his conversation. My feet feel the pedals on the floor. There's three of them–the accelerator, the brake, and the clutch. I could drive stick shift in high school, but I haven't operated a manual car in well over a decade. Heck, I haven't driven a normal automatic car in years. How am I supposed to pull this off?

The prince is still shouting at someone on his phone. Now is my chance to escape. I listen to my dad's voice in my head, calmly coaching me to make sure the car is in neutral and push the clutch in before turning the ignition. Letting out a silent cheer when it turns on, I manage to get the car into first gear and inch forward. Slowly weaving around the other vehicles parked in the garage, I head toward the exit.

The door of the stairwell swings open as I'm about to make a sharp turn onto the ramp. I hear the prince yelling at me to stop. Glancing down at Joshua to make sure he's still safely nestled in the passenger seat, I rapidly shift gears and speed up.

"Don't stall, don't stall," I plead with the car as I accelerate. Then when I see the garage door leading to the street is closed, I start to panic.

Hah. Who am I kidding? *Start* panicking? I've been panicking all along. What I really start doing is screaming at the top of my lungs. "Open, door, open!" If I have to brake to wait for the door to open, I'm not sure I'll get it going again. To make matters worse, I hear the prince's feet pounding on the cement as he runs up the ramp. He's yelling my name, which means he knows I'm the one behind the wheel.

I scream again at the garage door, this time with some more colorful language thrown in. Maybe the swear words are what did the trick because the door rolls open. Okay, it could have been the sensors detecting my vehicle, but honestly, who cares? I've escaped.

Turning onto the street in front of the prince's villa, I spot Asger standing on the sidewalk next to the getaway car, waving his arms in the air. I glance behind me to see if the prince is still in pursuit, but he's vanished. Coming to a stop, I take the car out of gear, put the parking brake on, and start to get out, but Asger tells me to stay put.

"We don't have time to switch drivers." He gets into the passenger seat, places my violin on his lap, then says urgently, "Go. Another car just pulled out of the garage."

As I speed down the street, I ask, "Where's Pedro?"

"There was someone on the roof of the prince's villa. We're pretty sure it was Hamish making his escape. Pedro went to track down Hamish, and I waited for you. We'll rendezvous later." Asger twists in his seat. "There's a red sports car behind us. It's the prince. Quick, make a left here."

I turn sharply into an alley, knocking over a couple of trash cans as I straighten up the wheel. Fortunately, that buys us a little breathing room since the prince has to stop his car to move the obstacles out of his way.

"We can't go back to HQ," I say. "The prince knows I have the violin. That will be the first place he looks."

"Just keep driving. Right now, we have to lose the prince. Then we'll figure out what to do next."

When I reach the end of the alley, I have to decide quickly which way to go. To the right? Or the left? I turn right and instantly regret that decision.

"Watch out," Asger yells as I narrowly miss smacking into a van.

"Is he still behind us?" I ask.

"Yes, turn here." As I fumble with the gearshift, Asger adds, "You're doing a great job, by the way. If you ever give up playing the violin, you could try your hand at Formula 1."

"Is Joshua okay?" We're on a busy road now, so I'm scared to take my eyes off the cars in front of me to check on my violin.

"He's fine," Asger reassures me. "Change lanes. See if you can lose him."

I weave back and forth in the traffic, earning angry stares from other drivers as they honk their horns. My stomach lurches as I run a red light. "This isn't working."

"Go left. Now." When I crank the wheel, Asger gasps. "No, I meant right. This is the sidewalk."

We both scream in unison as pedestrians scatter. I try to maneuver back into traffic, but when I see a police car with its sirens on, I freak out, turning the car sharply in the other direction.

Now everyone is screaming–me, Asger, and all the people on the steps. Yep, you heard that right–the steps. Not a road, alleyway, or even a sidewalk. The car is going down *steps.Actual* steps leading down to a plaza.

"Thud, thud, thud" rings in my ears as the car takes each step in turn. Then a brief respite as we roll across a landing. More "thud, thud, thud" as we go down another flight of steps. Now, there's a loud whacking noise as the driver's side of the car swipes a wrought-iron lamppost. A "clunk" as the side mirror tumbles to the ground. More screaming. Most of the cries and yells are coming from humans, but it's possible some of the screams are coming from my violin. Let's face it, even an inanimate musical instrument would be fearing for its life right about now.

Now, there's a sudden silence. No, wait a minute, it's not really a silence. More of a pleasant bubbling noise, like the sound fountains make . . . oh, crap. It *is* a fountain. A gorgeous, tiled fountain with a mermaid sculpture in the middle and we're heading directly toward it.

"Hit the brakes," Asger yells.

Suddenly, my feet don't know what to do anymore. Which one of these pedals is the brake? Which one is the accelerator? Oh, yeah, there's a clutch somewhere down there. I press on all of them, praying one of these is going to do the trick. Then the car stalls, but not in time.

Asger yells at me again. "Jump out of the car."

Pushing the door open, and grateful that I never put the seatbelt on in the first place, I do a very awkward dive and roll onto the ground. As I get to my feet, I watch the front end of the Citroën crumple as it smacks into the fountain.

My heart pounds as I look for Asger. Is he okay? Did he make it out of the car in time? A huge crowd has materialized, and I don't see anyone who looks like my Viking cowboy anywhere. Yelling out his name, I push through the throngs of people, then breathe a sigh of relief when I see a man wearing a Dolly Parton t-shirt sitting on a bench, my violin on his lap.

"Are you okay?" I call out as I rush toward him.

"Don't worry, Joshua is fine." He shakes his head. "I don't know how he survived that, but he did. It's a miracle."

I sit down next to Asger and stroke his arm. "I don't care about Joshua."

He grins. "Well, we both know that's not true."

As Asger hands my violin to me, I concede his

point. "Okay, Joshua is important to me. But you're more important."

I lean in to kiss him, but he stops me. "We should get out of here before the prince finds us."

"Oh, my gosh, your ankle," I say when Asger stands and grimaces.

"Which one?" he says wryly. "I think I twisted the other one with that last maneuver."

"So, stuntman isn't on your career list anymore?" I say in a moment of levity that's totally incongruent with the situation we're in.

Asger chuckles. "This is why I love being with you so much. You make me laugh when I need it the most."

I smile back at him, then say, "Come on, we need to get going."

Asger slings his arm around my shoulders and I help him walk across the plaza. People are staring and pointing at us, but thankfully no one tries to stop us from fleeing-or rather, hobbling-away from the scene.

It takes a while, but we finally make it to the street. Asger is leaning against a bus stop sign while I'm trying to hail a taxi. As I'm waving one down, I feel something sharp poking into my side. I gasp when I see that it's a knife. Then I stifle a scream when I realize who's holding it.

"Back away or the girl gets it," I hear the prince say to Asger.

Before Asger can do something stupid, I toss my violin into his hands. "Protect Joshua, okay? I'll be fine."

Asger reluctantly takes a few steps back, holding the violin close to his chest.

"Okay, here's what we're going to do," the prince says to Asger. "You're going to give me the violin, then I'll let Jasmine go. Or should we call her Terese? After all, that's who she was impersonating when you and your band performed in the preliminary round of the Riviera Musical Rodeo."

When I squirm, the prince grasps me around my waist, making sure I can feel the tip of the knife poking through the material of my top.

"It's a shame really that you broke the rules of the competition. *My* competition," the prince says coldly. "Whisky and Bragi was great. You stood a good chance of winning the finals and getting that recording contract. But of course, rules are rules, and now you have to be eliminated."

"Rules," I spit out. "You don't respect rules. If you did, you wouldn't have stolen my violin."

"I offered to buy it from you," the prince says. "It was your choice to do this the hard way."

I look down at the pavement, my stomach clenching. Asger's dreams of becoming a country music star are being crushed, all because of this vile man.

The prince's breath is hot on my neck, making my

skin crawl. "You've made things very difficult for me," he says. "You crashed my car into a fountain. The police are going to ask me a lot of awkward questions about what happened. I can't have people finding out you were able to break into my house and drive out with one of my cars. It would ruin my reputation. This is going to cost me a lot of money to hush up."

"But you're rich," I say dryly. "Money doesn't mean anything to you."

"It's the principle," he says.

"Oh, yeah, you're such a man of principle." I snort. "Sure, you may end up getting my violin in the end, but don't think I'm not going to make your life miserable. I'll tell every reporter I can find how you stole Joshua from me. Then let's see what happens to your reputation."

The prince sighs. "You really are going to be a lot of trouble, aren't you? I have more money and influence than you. What should we start with? Getting you deported? Sound good? How about kissing your career goodbye? And your boyfriend? Not only is he out of my competition, I'll make sure no one in the country music world wants anything to do with him."

My breath hitches as a tear rolls down my cheek. "All this because of my violin?"

"I always get what I want," he says. "No matter what the cost."

I repeat the prince's words over and over in my head–no matter what the cost. Then I say in a sweet voice, "I think I have an idea you'll like."

* * *

A few days later, I'm standing with the other members of Whiskey and Bragi backstage at the Rainier III Auditorium. It's the finals of the Riviera Musical Rodeo, and no one is more surprised than I am that we're about to go on stage and perform.

Okay, actually, there is one person more surprised than me. That's Asger. He's asking me for the millionth time how I convinced Prince Oboroten to give me back my violin and allow Whiskey and Bragi to compete.

"What did you say to him?" Asger asks. "Why did he agree?"

For the millionth time, I repeat my same answer. "I just reasoned with him. Once I explained to him that a Stradivarius or a Guarneri would be worth way more money than my silly Australian Avestruz, he saw the logic in that."

Asger shakes his head. "I still don't believe it."

"We're here, aren't we?" I motion at the stage. "The prince wouldn't have allowed us to play in the finals otherwise, right?"

"Shush," J.B. says to us. "They're about to announce us."

We step aside while the guys from Mrs. Moto & Co walk off stage. I have to admit, their set was great, but Whiskey and Bragi are hungrier for it. And given all the hurdles we've gone through to get to this point, I'm convinced we'll hit it out of the park.

As the emcee introduces us, I gently cradle my violin in my arms, whispering, "Ready to play some fiddle, Joshua?"

The noise from the crowd is deafening. It takes me a while to realize what they're chanting–"Viking cowboys, Viking cowboys, Viking cowboys." I look at J.B., Raphael, and Asger's Barbie-pink cowboy outfits and cowboy hats with horns and grin. It's definitely an unforgettable look. One that's going to take the country music world by storm.

As I tuck my violin under my chin, I feel butterflies in my stomach. This is it–do or die. After a few hesitant notes on my strings, I ease into the performance, reveling in the music. By the time we get to our final song, the crowd is on their feet. And when the last note is played, I know without a doubt that Whiskey and Bragi are going to win this.

Of course, there's the agonizing wait until the judges make their final decision. Asger paces back and forth, J.B. closes his eyes while he mutters a prayer, and Raphael stands stock-still with his fingers crossed.

When we're called back on stage with the other two bands, and Whiskey and Bragi is officially crowned as the winners of the first annual Riviera Musical Rodeo, Asger picks me up and spins me around.

As he lowers me to the ground, he kisses me lightly on the lips. "If there weren't all these people watching us, this kiss would last a lot longer," he says, his voice husky in my ear. "I love you, Jasmine."

My eyes water, then I pull his head toward me, giving him a kiss that lets him know I don't care we're in front of an audience. When we pull apart, I give Asger a gentle smile. "I love you, too."

After the onstage festivities are complete, we head down to the greenroom. But before I can go inside, Prince Oboroten appears and pulls me aside.

"Go on ahead," I say to the guys. "I'll be there in a sec."

"Are you sure?" Asger says.

I nod. "Yep, I'm fine."

Once Asger follows J.B. and Raphael into the greenroom, the prince smiles at me. It's a cold, calculating smile, one that doesn't reach his eyes. "Well, I've held up my end of the bargain. Now, it's your turn."

I take a deep breath, steeling myself for what needs to happen now. Then I hand my violin to the prince. In exchange, he hands me a five Euro note.

"See, selling your violin to me wasn't so hard," the prince says. "And you were right. It's much easier this way. I don't have to hide it away because our transaction was aboveboard and legal. You sold me your violin for five Euros."

My eyes water and I drop my gaze to the floor.

The prince sneers, "Actually, I gave you more than money for it, didn't I? I let your boyfriend and his band compete in the finals tonight. Women like you are so stupid. You'll do anything for love. Just wait until he makes it big and dumps you."

Suddenly, I feel calm and at peace. Unlike before, starting with Corey in high school, the losers I dated after that, and the jerk who conned me out of all my money, now I know with utter certainty that I've finally found a man who's worthy of me. One I can trust completely. One who I'd sacrifice my most prized possession for. My Viking cowboy Asger.

And with that knowledge, I turn on my heel and walk away from the prince and from Joshua for good.

* * *

The following week, Asger and I are cuddled up on the couch in the music room at Sebastien's villa, looking at pictures of violins for sale on my phone. When he found out about the deal I had made with the prince–my violin in exchange for Whiskey and Bragi not being disqualified from the Riviera Musical Rodeo–he went through a lot of emotions.

I pointed out that it had been my decision to make, and it was one I would make again. That wasn't easy for Asger to accept, but he made his peace with it. He still wanted to storm the prince's villa, confront him, and get my violin back. But after a private conversation with Sebastien, Asger backed down.

As I'm discussing the merits of a violin for sale in Austria with Asger, Sebastien bursts into the room and thrusts his tablet in my hands.

"Wait until you see this," Sebastien says.

I furrow my brow at the news program that's streaming. "Hey, isn't that the–"

"That's the prince's villa," Asger says, interrupting me.

Sebastien leans over and unmutes the broadcast so we can hear the reporter describing how Interpol has discovered a cache of priceless stolen goods at a private residence in Monte Carlo. Next, they cut to footage of uniformed agents in the prince's gallery. The camera sweeps around as the reporter describes various items on display.

"This painting was stolen from the Louvre," the reporter is saying. Then, as the camera pans through the room where the prince displayed his musical plunder, I gasp. The harpsichord is still there, but there's nothing on the velvet pillow where my violin had been displayed.

"Where's Joshua?" I yell at the screen.

"Excuse me, madam." I look up and see Sebastien's housekeeper standing there, a wedding band twinkling on one hand and a violin case clasped in her other. "This was just delivered for you."

She smiles as she sets the violin case on the coffee table. Attached to it is a small envelope. I tear it open and pull out an ivory card, which simply reads, "He missed you. H."

"H?" I tilt my head. "What does 'H' mean?"

"Open it up," Sebastien suggests.

My hands tremble as I undo the clasps on the violin case. I slowly lift the lid, then a smile spreads across my face. "Joshua," I say softly. "I did miss you."

Then I look over at Asger and he's grinning ear-to-ear. I turn to Sebastien and he's got the same expression. "Hey, wait a minute. Did you guys know about this? Is that what your private conversation was about?"

Sebastien shrugs. "Hypothetically speaking, Hamish might have alerted his contact in Interpol about Obie's gallery and his contact might have made sure Hamish retrieved a certain violin before they raided the place."

"Aren't hypotheticals fun?" Asger says to me. "Now, hypothetically speaking, how do you feel about continuing to play fiddle with Whiskey and Bragi?"

"Not gonna happen, man," Sebastien says to him. "She's sticking with the quartet."

While the two of them continue to have a mock argument about which musical group I'm going to play with, I take Joshua out of his case, walk over to the window, and start to play.

EPILOGUE – ASGER
(FOUR YEARS LATER)

"There's someone at the door," Jasmine yells out from the bathroom. "Can you get it? I just got out of the shower."

I set my guitar down, smiling at my wife's ability to hear a knock on the door even when she's at the other end of the apartment. Walking from our small music room to the foyer, I almost trip over our recently adopted cat.

"Are you sure that's the best place to take a nap, Dolly?"

The look in Dolly's green eyes lets me know she'll sleep wherever she wants, thank you very much. I step over the fluffy Persian, then open the front door.

"Are you Asger Christensen? Sign here," the delivery man says as he hands me a tablet. After I scrawl my name, he jabs a finger at a large flat box leaning up against the wall of the corridor. "All yours."

"What is it?" I call out after the man's retreating back, but he just grunts in reply.

As I'm dragging the box inside, Jasmine pads down the hall, a terry-cloth robe cinched around her waist. As she dries off her long dark hair with a towel, she says, "Oh, good. It's here."

"What is it?" I ask.

She grins. "A surprise. Can you take it into the guest room? I'll be there in a minute."

Grunting as I hoist the box up, I wonder what Jasmine has ordered this time. Ever since we moved into this apartment in Monte Carlo a few months ago, she's been in full-on decorating mode, telling me she wants this place to feel like a real home, not a soulless place we crash at when we got a spare moment.

As usual, she's right. The past four years have been a whirlwind. Ever since Whiskey and Bragi won the Riviera Musical Rodeo, recorded our first album, and hit the charts, it's been non-stop. First it was our North American tour, then a worldwide tour, followed by another album, red carpet appearances at all the awards shows, more recording, more sell-out concerts . . . just thinking about it makes me exhausted.

Of course, Jasmine has been just as busy. Despite trying to persuade her to become Whiskey and Bragi's permanent fiddler, classical music was always her first love. The Fjura Quartet continued to perform in all corners of the globe until last year, when they made the bittersweet decision to part ways. It had been one of those moments when they realized they all had different paths to follow, but would always remain the best of friends.

Pedro had decided to return to Mexico and open the first official branch of the Musical Detectives Agency. It turns out there are other musicians in need of private investigators, and Pedro was excited to hang up his shingle and help solve musical crimes. He didn't go alone, though. Grace was right there by his side, having, much to her surprise, fallen in love with Pedro.

Realizing that there are only so many superyachts and polo ponies a man needs, Sebastien had put his vast fortune to good use, setting up a charity to provide instruments and lessons to children who otherwise couldn't afford them.

My sweet Jasmine struck out on her own, becoming a solo violinist. At first, she didn't believe she had the talent to be a featured artist rather than a member of a quartet or orchestra. But Joshua helped build up her confidence, inspiring her to spread her wings.

Yes, Joshua. Not the violin, Joshua, but the real-life Joshua Bell. When he heard through the musical grapevine how his namesake violin had been stolen, and then recovered by a mysterious ex-cat burglar, he insisted on meeting Jasmine. After coaxing her into playing for him, he was so impressed by her musical abilities that he helped her land her first solo gig. After that, it was all down to Jasmine, and she flourished.

With all that's been going on, it's a wonder we found time to get married. But I'm so glad we did. These past six months have been the happiest of my life.

"What are you daydreaming about?" Jasmine asks, interrupting my thoughts. She's leaning against the door of the guest room, clad in leggings and a loose top, her hair hanging loosely around her shoulders.

"Just how lucky I am," I say. Then I set the cardboard box on the floor and inspect it. "Hey, wait a minute. This is from my family's company. Why are they sending us flat-pack furniture?"

Jasmine motions around the empty room. "It's high time we furnished this, don't you think?"

"We decided on two twin beds and a dresser, didn't we?" I furrow my brow. "This box doesn't look big enough to hold either of those."

"Why don't you open it up?" she suggests, handing me a utility knife.

As I slice through the top of the box, I point out that my family's flat-pack business is a luxury one. "They send someone to assemble the furniture. There won't be any instructions in here."

She chuckles. "Your mom thought you could handle this on your own."

"What is this, anyway?" I ask as I pull out the various pieces of wood and fasteners. When Jasmine shrugs, I look on the side of the box for the model name, then my eyes widen. "Is this what I think it is?"

Jasmine rubs her belly gently as I leap to my feet. "Instead of setting this room up as a guest bedroom, don't you think a nursery would be a better idea?"

I pull Jasmine into my arms, embracing her . . . no, wait a minute . . . embracing the two of them. I try to speak, but words fail me. Finally, I manage to splutter, "When?"

"In about eight months," she says. "Just enough time for you to figure out how to assemble this crib."

AUTHOR'S NOTE

Thank you so much for reading *Smitten with Caviar*! If you enjoyed it, I'd be grateful if you would consider leaving a short review on Goodreads and/or your favorite retailer. Reviews help other readers find my books and encourage me to keep writing.

When my husband and I visited Monaco many years ago, the Grand Prix had just taken place. Although we didn't get to see the Formula 1 drivers racing through the streets of Monte Carlo, it was really neat to see how the course was laid out. We also enjoyed touring the casino and exploring other parts of this beautiful principality. That trip, along with my love of classical music, inspired me to write this book. And, of course, I had to throw in references to two of my musical idols—Joshua Bell and Dolly Parton.

As always, it's so much fun to weave in little Easter eggs and references to other books in this series, as well as my other series. The band called Mrs. Moto & Co is a nod to my Mollie McGhie cozy mystery series which stars the fabulous feline, Mrs. Moto, and Hamish MacDougall played a big role in *Smitten with Strudel*. Spoiler alert: he and Celeste are going to be the main characters in one of my future Smitten with Travel books. I can't wait to write their own happily-ever-after!

I did take liberties with a few things in this book, such as the description of the casino and the auditorium. Jasmine's Avestruz violin is completely made up. Although, wouldn't it be cool if there was a violin with koala and kangaroo engravings on it? And Joshua Bell's slimy personal assistant, who conned Jasmine out of her money? Thank goodness, he's completely fictitious.

If you'd like to know when I have a new release, find out about sales/promos, and get other updates, you can sign up for my newsletter to stay in touch - subscribepage.com/m4g9m4

ABOUT THE AUTHOR

Ellen Jacobson is a chocolate obsessed cat lover who writes cozy mysteries and romantic comedies. After working in Scotland and New Zealand for several years, she returned to the States, lived aboard a sailboat, traveled around in a tiny camper, and is now settled in a small town in northern Oregon with her husband and an imaginary cat named Simon.

Find out more at ellenjacobsonauthor.com

ALSO BY ELLEN JACOBSON

Smitten with Travel Romantic Comedies

Smitten with Ravioli
Smitten with Croissants
Smitten with Strudel
Smitten with Candy Canes
Smitten with Baklava
Smitten with Caviar

Mollie McGhie Mysteries

Robbery at the Roller Derby
Murder at the Marina
Bodies in the Boatyard
Poisoned by the Pier
Buried by the Beach
Dead in the Dinghy
Shooting by the Sea
Overboard on the Ocean
Murder Aboard the Mistletoe

North Dakota Library Mysteries

Planning for Murder
Murder at the Library
Poisoned by the Book